"I've learned things from working with you, Kathryn."

He was standing so close her folded arms were sandwiched between them.

Kathryn pushed her hair back from her forehead. The heat emanating from Sledge seemed suddenly overwhelming. "All right," she said, trying to look composed. "What do you think you've learned?"

"That when a woman keeps pushing her hair back the way you do, she's preening."

"I'm not!"

"Right," he said with a wink. "And your pupils are the size of dimes. In your book you said pupils dilate when they see something they like." He followed her down as she sank onto the sofa. "Explain that one."

"The lights are dim," she argued as his face moved closer to hers. "Your pupils are enlarged, too."

"I don't doubt it," he whispered. "And I don't deny the reason, either."

Tracy Hughes, the daughter of a U.S. Air Force colonel, became accustomed to having her roots spread all over the globe with her family's frequent moves during her childhood. Now that she is married with a young daughter, she still finds she loves to travel. In between winter skiing trips to Colorado and summer beachcombing trips to Florida or Mississippi with her family, this talented author finds time in her busy writing schedule to meet romance readers and attend as many writers' conferences as possible.

Books by Tracy Hughes

HARLEQUIN ROMANCE
2744—QUIET LIGHTNING

Impressions
Tracy Hughes

Harlequin Books

TORONTO • NEW YORK • LONDON
AMSTERDAM • PARIS • SYDNEY • HAMBURG
STOCKHOLM • ATHENS • TOKYO • MILAN

ISBN 0-373-02792-3

Harlequin Romance first edition October 1986

For Penny Richards,
who picks me up and dusts me off time after time.

Printed in U.S.A.

CHAPTER ONE

THE RECORDED SOUND of Mick Jagger's cocky vocals filled the dimly lit room, lending a note of anonymity to the laughing, flirting voices. Warm, humorous memories assaulted Kathryn Ellerbee as she stepped into the mainstream of the social activity and made a quick pan of the Manhattan club—the ceiling fans twirling overhead, the glass booth housing the disk jockey, the red-hued lighting, the animated faces of people on the prowl. Several pairs of eyes swept over her, darted away, moved back. Self-consciously bringing a hand up to the long brown spiral curls that cascaded over her shoulders, Kathryn scanned the faces for the one she had come to see. "He's usually at the left end of the bar," she'd been told that morning. "Goes there to unwind every day after work."

Squinting through the haze of smoke and people, Kathryn took inventory of the men at the bar—a sales type in a wash-and-wear suit, a fraternity row escapee, a sheep in wolf's clothing. But her stereotyping came to an end when she saw the breathtaking, tall and tanned form of the man she had been seeking, leaning back against the bar, his black hair the perfect foil for penetrating blue eyes that riveted directly on hers. The impact of his seductive scrutiny shook her off balance, reminding her that she had intended not to be noticed.

She wrenched her eyes away, located a vacant table near the back and made her way toward it. Sitting so that he was directly in her line of vision, Kathryn motioned for a barmaid and ordered two drinks—a ginger ale for herself and a beer for the empty chair next to her—just to throw off potential Casanovas who might drift her way. Deliberately she kept her eyes off the intriguing man at the bar until she had the security of a glass at her lips. Then, taking a sip, she stole a glance over the rim. He had changed positions. His body was now angled toward the bar, with one elbow resting on it, as if the territory were roped off, reserved only for him. Darryl Sledge, commonly known to his co-workers and friends simply as "Sledge," sat with one foot resting easily on the rung of his stool, so that his relaxed body looked comfortable and unaffected. His absorption in the folded newspaper he held gave the appearance that he was harmless, as if his last thought were on hunting down available women. But his heart-stopping blue eyes, as they moved back and forth across the page, told her without a doubt that he could be very dangerous, indeed.

A puzzled frown drew her brows together, and Kathryn reached in her purse and pulled out a small notebook and pen. This was not the aggressive, domineering, intimidating Darryl Sledge she had been watching in the taped interviews he'd done for the pilot being prepared for the news program *InSight*. As a matter of fact, she mused, sensuality radiated from him and drew involuntary glances from women all over the room. Was it the disheveled look of his black hair that made him so attractive, the rugged tan, or the thick, dark brown mustache calling attention to his full mouth? Or was it the way he wore his shirt, open for a few buttons, revealing the dark curls on his chest, as if he'd just slung off his jacket and tie and left them lying somewhere?

Whatever it was that made him so appealing, she thought analytically, it worked. She watched the women brushing past him, leaning across him to order drinks, sending him piercing looks. The hint of a grin working at his eyes told her that he was quite aware of his magnetism and was merely biding his time until he chose his prey.

Shaking her head to break free from his subtle power, Kathryn picked up her notebook and tried to jot down his actions.

She glanced back up at him and caught her breath. Those blue eyes were on her again, holding her gaze seconds longer than necessary before moving away to scan the rest of the crowd. Heat flushed Kathryn's cheeks in reaction to the brief connection, and she silently rebuked herself for her involuntary response to moves that should no longer work on her. Looking away, she tried to remind herself of why she was here, but it wasn't long before she felt the intensity of his gaze burning into her again. She met his eyes and brought her drink to her lips, sipping the beverage to help calm nerves he had frayed with one look. His mustache tipped upward in an acknowledging smile, and he dropped his gaze to his paper again.

Breathing easier at the momentary reprieve, Kathryn set her notebook in her lap and stared down at the blank page. The jumbled impressions he'd just given her in capsule were too convoluted to write down. Annoyed at herself for not being able to keep her professional cool, she nibbled her lip and studied him.

Her heart bolted when he glanced up at her again, and she watched, mesmerized, as he laid his newspaper on the bar and stood up. With a surge of disappointment, she wondered if he was leaving. But the answer came as he picked up his drink and sauntered toward her.

A surprised smile struggled to form on her face, but she deliberately held it back. Her mouth went dry as he stood grinning at her from across the table. His eyes were so direct, so bold, so penetrating, that she found herself unable to look away. Slowly, hypnotically, he leaned across the table, bracing himself on bent arms, until his face was no more than inches away from hers. "Thought you might want a closer look," he drawled in a deep voice that went through her with more force than the bass guitar vibrating through the speakers.

Completely original, if a little arrogant, she thought as amusement sparkled in her eyes. Determined not to wilt under his directness, she chose an honest approach. "That's what I came here for," she returned.

His arched brows told her he was surprised by her quick comeback, and he straightened up and pulled out the chair next to her, where the tepid beer still sat. Without asking permission, he lowered himself into the chair, crossed an ankle over his knee and set his drink down. He nodded toward the untouched beer. "Did you order that for me?"

Kathryn folded her arms on the table and leaned toward him. "How do you know I don't have a two-hundred-pound boyfriend heading this way?"

"If you do, you've either been stood up or ignored since you got here. Neither seems likely. So my guess is that you ordered the beer to fend off admirers."

"The same way you use your newspaper."

A grin worked its way across his face, revealing perfect teeth that looked so white against his dark complexion. "Very perceptive."

"Tell me," Kathryn said, picking up her glass and absently tracing the rim with a finger. "Why is it that my ploy worked on everyone but you?"

"Because you couldn't keep your eyes off me," he said matter-of-factly in an unflappable Texas drawl. "Not since you walked in."

His cockiness placed them at a stalemate, and since she was not ready to reveal her purpose for watching him, she simply sipped her ginger ale and shook her head. Sledge leaned back with a smile, bottomed his drink and watched her as her quiet laughter died away. Pointing toward the beer, she said, "Go ahead and drink it. There's no use wasting it."

Sledge leaned forward and curled his fingers over hers. "I'd rather share yours," he said, bringing her glass, still encased in her hand, to his lips. Kathryn's heart beat out an unhealthy rhythm as his eyes met hers over the rim of the glass. *This guy has moves that even I haven't documented,* she thought with disbelief.

"Ginger ale?" he rumbled, setting the glass down, but keeping his hand over hers. "Trying to keep your wits about you?"

"Sometimes it pays."

"I see your point," he said with a seductive slant to his mouth that would have melted her if she hadn't forced herself to remember what she knew about such smiles. "Then you can drive us home."

"Home?"

"My home, your home. Wherever."

Kathryn disengaged her hand from his and set it in her lap. "You don't even know my name," she told him.

"Details," he said, cocking his head. "It's not your name I want to take home."

Certain that it was time to cut the evening short before things went farther, Kathryn reached for her purse, shoved her notebook inside and clicked it shut. "Well," she said with a sigh, "I guess that's all academic, since you aren't going to take me or my name home with you tonight."

Sledge lifted a long curl of her hair, wound it around his finger and inched closer as if the strand were drawing him toward her. "You aren't one of those women who like to pretend they're tricked into going home with a man, are you? I thought honesty would be my best bet.''

"Honesty is good," Kathryn said, trying to ignore the allure of his clean breath on her face, the roughness of his hand as it nuzzled her neck, the subtle pressure of his calf touching hers. "But believe me, you'd hate yourself in the morning."

Sledge glanced up at the ceiling and shook his head. "Impossible."

"Just the same," she maintained, "I intend to go home alone."

"Right," he said without conviction, feathering the strand of her hair between his fingers. "At least let me walk you to your car, then."

"No," she said. Men like him always expected to change a woman's mind under the intimate night sky. "I'm not afraid to walk to the parking lot alone."

"Just to humor my ego?" he pressed.

Kathryn couldn't help but answer his persuasive grin. "Your ego doesn't need any help."

"It will if I let you walk out of here alone."

Blowing out a defeated breath, Kathryn assessed the determined look on his face, the compelling eyes that shook her resolve. Fighting him was futile. "All right," she decided. "Walk me to my car, but no farther."

Sledge eyed his watch and stood up. "Let's see. That should give me a good three minutes to make my move."

"I thought you'd already made it."

"That was just preamble," he said, and extended his hand as if she needed help to stand. "I can't try the real thing in public."

Kathryn hesitated when he slid his hand up her forearm and started to walk. "I don't think—"

"I promise to keep my hands to myself," he reassured her in a chuckling voice. "My methods are strictly psychological."

Kathryn tried to appear undaunted as they neared the front of the club. "Should you be telling me this? Aren't you afraid of disclosing your secrets?"

"Not a bit," he said, giving a distressing thumbs-up sign to the bouncer and holding the glass door open for Kathryn. "Awareness is no defense against my techniques."

A laugh stole up from Kathryn's throat. "You're pretty sure of yourself, aren't you?"

"Pretty sure," he conceded with a teasing leer. He let go of her arm and slid his hands into his pockets as they left the noise behind them. The warm June breeze whispered through his hair, leaving it even more becomingly tousled than it had been in the bar. Silence connected them as he gazed down at her, his watchful eyes fanning the anticipation smoldering within her. He was not going to let her get in her car and drive away, she realized, and she was beginning to look forward to his methods for stopping her.

Another breeze whipped around them, carrying the faintest scent of an exotic but popular cologne that sensitized her even more. The club's bright sign, Steppin' Out, flashed overhead like a beacon, giving an orange glow to the parking lot spread out before them. Sledge was making his move already, she realized. The way he refrained from touching her, his innocent study of the pavement, the bent position of his arms, were all signals designed to create an aura of vulnerability. But she knew from her research that those signs were the ones to guard against.

She'd have to tell him who she was. It was the only way. It was best to spring it on him now, so that when she had to start working with him the next day, her identity wouldn't be a negative surprise. At her car she opened the door and tossed her purse on the seat. Turning to face him, she saw further evidence of his technique.

His eyes grew more serious in their assessment of her. He kept his hands in his pockets, and on his face there was no trace of the smile she had seen there earlier. She couldn't move as he wet his lips, kept them parted, inclined his head slightly and began lowering his face to hers in degrees so minute that she sensed more than saw what was happening.

"I have to tell you who I am before..." she whispered, her voice trailing off.

"Before what?" he asked, his lips as close as they could be without touching hers.

Her breath was taking on a new rhythm, deeper and faster. "Before this goes any further."

"Fine," he murmured, as if her words guaranteed surrender. "Tell me."

"I'm Kathryn—"

"Hi, Kathryn," he cut in, and then his lips brushed hers, soft and moist, stirring dormant, ancient fires within her. Neither his body nor his hands touched her as he coaxed her lips apart. His tongue met hers tentatively in sweet swirling persuasion. She felt the pressure of his kiss increase, felt his breath breeze harder against her lips, felt her heart struggling for full rein, but still he kept his body apart from hers. Warm wind whipped her hair around his face, but she didn't notice. The door to the bar opened and laughter spilled out, but she didn't notice. Her knees trembled beneath her weight, but she didn't notice. Finally, with one last enticement from his tongue, he pulled back, brushed his lips over hers again and ended the kiss.

"How am I doing?" he whispered.

"Good," Kathryn said, swallowing to regain her composure, ordering her galloping heart to slow. "But I have to tell you who I am before this gets—"

"Out of hand?" he provided. "Mmm. Sounds intriguing." His lips hovered near hers again, threatening deeper involvement.

"You don't understand," she said in a hoarse whisper. "I'm Kathryn Ellerbee."

"Hi, Kathryn Ellerbee," he said. His lips crushed hers, and a frustrated sigh escaped from her mouth, only to be breathed in by his. His body made contact this time, the hard warmth of his chest brushing against her breasts, the strain and pull of his muscles belying his relaxed stance, hands still in his pockets. She felt him shudder, felt his heart slamming against her breast, felt the whisper of a moan vibrate in his throat. When he broke the kiss, his mustache brushed her cheek. "You want to go for the middle name?" he asked.

Kathryn closed her eyes, realizing she was sinking deeper and deeper with each kiss. "I'm Kathryn Ellerbee," she repeated earnestly, before she could change her mind, "the image consultant."

"Image...?" The word died, along with the desire that had heightened his features. "The one they hired to...?"

"Help you with your image," she finished, feeling a sudden rush of cold when he stepped back.

His eyes took on a razor sharpness, the same glint she had seen in his tapes, the hardness she had been hired to erase. He set his hands on his hips, turned back toward the club. Compressing his lips, he asked, "So what were you doing here tonight? Spying on me? Gathering ammunition against me?"

Kathryn drew a hand through her hair. "No—yes. I've been studying your tapes, and I wanted one look at you off camera before I started working with you."

"You mean working *on* me, don't you?"

Kathryn dropped her hand from her hair, letting it fall like a veil over her face.

"You should have told me." The accusation grated out through his teeth.

"You're right. I should have. I handled things badly. But I didn't expect you to notice me when I came here tonight. I was trying to be discreet."

"You're about as discreet as a meteorite, with those big seductive eyes and that roll-out-of-bed hairdo. You think I don't know a come-hither look when I see it?"

"I'm the expert in body language, Sledge," she blurted. "Don't analyze my behavior to me."

"No, you're the one getting paid to analyze mine, huh?"

"Does that bother you?"

"Yes, it bothers me! I have a list of credentials so long it could lead you home, not to mention a photographic memory and the ability to see a story a mile away. The last thing I need is somebody like you riding in on the latest fad and telling me I don't sit right when I'm on camera."

"Your problems in front of the camera go deeper than the way you sit, Sledge, and your producer is concerned about your image off camera, as well. He made it very clear that you were hired under the condition that you work with me. He said you were good at your job, but if you're going to be on national television, he wants you more polished."

"And you're going to polish me?" he asked with a mirthless laugh. "A few minutes ago I didn't notice a whole lot of complaints about me."

"That has nothing to do with the job I was hired to do," Kathryn returned, berating herself for letting this go as far as it had.

"Just for the record, Miss Kathryn Ellerbee," he said, making her name sound ridiculous with his exaggerated articulation, "what is it that makes you think you can do anything for me?"

Kathryn folded her arms. "I have a list of credentials so long it could lead *you* home, by way of your nearest conquest's house. Besides having the complete faith of the network and contracts for a dozen of their top stars, I've worked with politicians I'm not at liberty to name, Olympic stars gone Hollywood, presidents of giant corporations—even royalty. My studies are documented in a best-selling book, *Gestures*, and I have degrees in psychology and anthropology. Would you like me to go on?"

"Sounds real impressive, but you didn't answer my question," he said, tipping his head back and peering down his nose at her. "What makes you think you can fix something that isn't broken?"

Ignoring the arrogant denial of his problems, Kathryn dropped her arms to her sides. "Unless you cooperate with me, I can't do anything for you. And if I don't help you, you'll lose your job before the pilot even airs. This doesn't have to be unpleasant. It can even be fun."

"Oh, yeah. Sounds like loads of fun."

"You have a bad attitude, Mr. Sledge."

He slung open her car door and gestured toward the seat. "Get in your car, Kathryn Ellerbee, and drive away. And when you show up in the morning with your little bag of tricks, I'll be just like a puppy waiting to be trained. In fact, I learn so fast, we might not have to spend much time together at all!"

Rolling her eyes heavenward at his sarcasm, Kathryn got into her car. "I'll see you tomorrow."

"Looking forward to it," he said, before slamming her door and striding off.

Kathryn cranked the car's engine and pulled out of the parking space, reminding herself of why she generally remained uninvolved with the irrational animal called man and why she had made a career out of figuring him out. Sledge's ego came as no surprise, for he was no different from any other client she'd ever had.

She would treat him like any other client, whether he liked it or not. And she would "fix" him if it killed her!

CHAPTER TWO

"THE MUSTACHE HAS TO GO," Louis Renfroe grumbled the next morning as he jotted down a list of his pet peeves concerning Darryl Sledge. "Too brown next to his black hair. Looks too bushy over his lip. Besides, viewers don't trust men with hair on their faces."

Although she had lain awake all night thinking of ways to improve Darryl Sledge, the idea of taking away his mustache was a bit distressing. Sliding to the edge of the Chippendale chair in the producer's office, she leaned forward and arched her brows pleadingly. "We could trim it back a little. Or dye it to match his hair."

"No. Too much is at stake. If this pilot isn't perfect, it could cost me my career. I think the ratings will be better without it. Shave it off."

Moaning within, Kathryn wrote "can the mustache" on her notepad, wondering if this would come as a complete shock to Sledge or if it had already been discussed. "Would you like to tell him, or shall I?"

The first hint of amusement she had ever seen on Renfroe's face broke through his gruff expression. "You tell him, but I'll watch. From a distance."

"Thanks a lot," Kathryn said, failing to see the humor. "That way if there's a casualty, it doesn't have to affect *InSight*'s budget, right?"

"There won't be any casualties," the red-haired man assured her, clasping his hands over his paunch. "Sledge is a sucker for a pretty smile. If anyone can get him into shape, you can."

Kathryn's shoulders sagged. "You know, Mr. Renfroe, if I'm going to help him at all, it would be best not to make this too painful. I think we should start with something easier and work up to the mustache."

"We don't have time. I want the mustache off today. He's taping some promo spots tomorrow, so I'll need all the external things like wardrobe and hair done immediately." His tone brooked no further debate.

"No problem," Kathryn said in feigned surrender. "Anything else?" *How about a quick nose job?* she thought sarcastically. *I know a doctor on the West Coast who can shorten his height a few inches.*

"Yeah. He's going to be in the limelight a lot when this show airs, so I want you to work hard on his private image as well as his public one. The playboy image isn't going to draw the kind of audience we want. We're doing a serious news program, and I want Sledge to be taken seriously."

Terrific, she thought. Her other assignment for the month was to turn a failing actor into a playboy to capture the public's attention. In her profession the ironies constantly surprised her.

A knock sounded on the door while she was considering how to accomplish her task. Without waiting for an invitation, Darryl Sledge opened the door and stepped inside. "You got a minute to—?" His voice faded when he saw Kathryn. He allowed her a tight smile and an acknowledging nod as he slipped his hands into the pockets of his gray corduroy trousers. Under the fluorescent overhead lights, his eyes looked paler than they had last night in darkness, and the lashes framing them were blacker than she had remembered.

With stiffened shoulders that were defined by the tight stretch of his white pullover, he faced his producer. "Sorry," he said in a cool tone. "I didn't realize I was interrupting a brainstorming. Did the two of you come up with any ideas to make me presentable?" The thin smile made his words seem less sarcastic, but his eyes pierced Kathryn with chilling intensity.

"Quite a few," Renfroe said, pulling himself slowly out of his chair. "Kathryn's done wonders with some others the network assigned to her, and I know she'll do a good job on you."

Sledge turned toward her and threw open his arms theatrically. "I'm putty," he said. "Mold away."

Folding her arms over the notepad she held against her chest, Kathryn matched his smug smile. "I intend to, Mr. Sledge. I intend to."

"Great. Where do we start? The eyes, the hands? They tell me I have a dazzling smile, but you might want to alter it a little so I don't give the ladies who watch my show palpitations."

"I think I have a pretty clear picture, Mr. Sledge," Kathryn said. "We won't have any problems finding a place to start. Besides, I love challenges."

"Then you'll enjoy the hell out of me," he drawled, eyes frosting. "When do we get started?"

"Immediately."

"Great!" he said with exaggerated zeal.

Renfroe clapped his thick hands together. "I like the enthusiasm, Sledge. Now you two get to work."

Kathryn tried to suppress her amusement at the aggravated smile plastered on Sledge's face as he led her down the hall to his dressing room. Mentally she went over the things she needed to take care of today. His clothes, his hair—his mustache.

Her smile lost some of its humor as she cast a side-long glance at the brown whiskers above his lips and recalled the feel of them when he'd kissed her. Unnecessary waste, she thought. The mustache gave him character. But she had been hired to do a job, and she would give the network what it wanted. The only problem was whether to tackle the mustache issue first or last.

"This is my dressing room," Sledge said, breaking the tense silence when they reached his unmarked door. He opened the door, and led her into the large earth-colored room arranged to resemble a studio apartment. "Feel free to redecorate if the urge strikes."

Kathryn threw him a frustrated look. "I'd say I already have my hands full, wouldn't you?" Letting out a sarcastic laugh in reply, Sledge dropped onto the sofa.

Kathryn disregarded him and made a quick visual sweep of the room, noting the overstuffed velvet sofa and love seat, the bar nestled discreetly in the corner, the swivel chair in front of a decidedly masculine vanity with lit mirrors. On the wall were several framed photos—one of him with the small news team he had worked with in Texas, a shot of him as a teenager with a friend in front of an old jalopy on which they had written Boston or Bust, a picture of him with a beautiful young woman whose arms encircled his waist.

Annoyance twisted inside her at the last photo, and she berated herself for taking the pose personally. Forcing herself to think in professional terms, she turned to see Sledge watching her, arms spanning the length of the sofa, waiting for her to fire the first shot in their inevitable battle of wills.

"May I go through your closets?" she asked finally.

After a moment of hesitation a genuine grin broke through his tight facade. "Damn, but you're nosy."

Kathryn couldn't help answering his grin. "Sorry. I didn't mean to be so blunt. Mr. Renfroe said you kept some of your clothes here, and he wants me to help you select a new wardrobe. I'd like to see what you've been wearing up till now."

Sledge's grin gave way to aggravation, and he raked a hand through his tousled hair. "Go ahead. Guess I ought to at least give you a point or two for asking first."

Kathryn opened the closet door and pushed back the clothes hanging on the rod. As she reached out to check the texture of one of the coats, her hand brushed something smooth at the back of the closet. She caught her breath and jumped back.

A life-size, cardboard image of Darryl Sledge, smiling his most lecherous smile, stared out at her.

Sledge's deep laughter calmed some of her surprise, and he stepped up behind her. "Don't look so scared. It's just me."

Reaching past her, he pulled out the stand-up portrait and propped it against the wall. Darryl Sledge, in all his cockiness, his mussed head tilted, his devilish grin in place, coaxed her to smile. His cardboard chest was bare, glistening with a thin sheen of perspiration, and his thumbs were hooked in the low-riding pockets of his worn jeans. One hand held a dusty black Stetson, and his feet, in battered Western-style boots, were crossed at the ankles. The real-life Sledge leaned against the wall beside his likeness. "Want one for yourself?" he asked. "Every red-blooded American woman should have one."

The heat of exasperation flushed Kathryn's cheeks, and she leaned against the back of the sofa and grimaced. "I've found some interesting things in my line of work, but I think this one might get the trophy."

"Might? You mean I have competition?"

Kathryn folded her arms as she remembered one case that rivaled this one. "I once found a woman sleeping in an actor's kitchen cupboards. It seems he had thrown a party the night before and thought he'd cleared everyone out."

"Well, you haven't even been to my house yet. Who knows what you'll find there?"

Kathryn wondered at the unhindered magnetism that came into play when his guard was down. "Did you plant the poster there for my benefit?"

Sledge laughed and set the cardboard figure back in his closet. "Wish I'd thought of it," he said. "But frankly, I'd forgotten it was there. My kid sister had it made for me when I moved up here a few months ago. She's got an expensive sense of humor. Worships me, but who can blame her?" Sledge strode across the room and indicated the woman in the photo. "That's her there."

"Your sister?" Kathryn asked quickly, a bit too much relief evident in her voice. "Oh, I thought—"

"She was one of my ladies?" He slumped back onto the sofa again. "No way. I'd be a fool to hang a picture of one of them on the wall. You never know which one might pop in."

"Good thinking," Kathryn said without inflection, bristling at the fact that last night she had almost made his list. Biting back her vexation, she went back to his closet to resume her study of his wardrobe.

An uneasy silence followed, until finally, in a tense voice, Sledge said, "Renfroe didn't mention that he had a problem with my clothes. Are there any other surprises?"

Kathryn's hand fell away from the tweed jacket she'd been examining, and she took a deep breath. Now was the time to deal with the mustache. Sledge's question had been direct, and she couldn't justify evading it. Turning around, she dropped her notepad on the table. "Yes, as a matter of fact there is one."

Sledge swallowed and propped his elbow on the back of the sofa. "All right, let's hear it."

Kathryn told herself to temper her voice with a conviction she did not feel. It never paid to let a subject know she didn't agree with the changes she was ordered to make. "It's your mustache. Renfroe wants you to shave it off."

A flash of fire shot through Sledge's eyes, but he didn't move a muscle. "He wants me to shave my mustache?" The words were spoken slowly, his tone teetering on the brink of being explosive. He raised a finger to his face. "*This* mustache?"

"Yes. He wants you polished from head to toe."

"I've had this mustache since I was eighteen years old in Vietnam," he bit out. "I've worn it on television for ten years."

"That was regional TV. You're in the big leagues now, Sledge," she said. "You have to play by their rules."

"Which include shaving my mustache."

"Yes."

He lowered his head, eyes darting from side to side, mouth clenched shut. "Polished." The word seemed to leave a bitter taste in his mouth.

"Yes."

Slowly he got up and went to the bathroom adjoining the dressing room. Kathryn stepped into the doorway behind him. She watched him lean over the sink and look solemnly in the mirror, stroking the thick slash of whiskers. "When?" he asked quietly.

Kathryn cleared her throat. "Today. Renfroe wants it off before you make the promo tapes. We—we could let the barber take care of it."

"No." He took a deep breath, turned away from the mirror. Anger twitched his nostrils, and a long, deep sigh tangled its way out of his lungs. "Damn!" he muttered, directing his frustration toward the ceiling. "Why do I want this job so much?"

"It's a good job, Sledge." Kathryn tried to ease the blow. "They're only asking you to shave your mustache."

"Would they like me to shave my head, too?" he railed. "I could have my chin tattooed with the network logo. I know—why don't we pierce my nose and put a permanent microphone there? That way they can make sure my image stays consistent all the time."

"You agreed to changes when you took the job."

"I agreed to *some* changes. I didn't think I'd put in months of work so they could turn around and slap me with this!" He stroked the whiskers again and glared furiously out the twentieth-floor window. "Whose idea was this, anyway? Yours?"

"Mr. Renfroe's."

"Then why didn't he mention it before?"

"Because he's a coward."

Her bluntness provided a vent for some of his tension, and his eyes lost their daggerlike intensity. "Well," he said, looking down onto the busy Manhattan streets below. "I could refuse, but I don't have anything on my side. Until the pilot airs, I can't really prove my worth, can I?"

"Not statistically," Kathryn agreed quietly.

"All right," he conceded, opening his palms as he turned back to her. "What choice do I have? I surrender."

Kathryn swallowed. "Do you want to shave it now, or wait until later today?"

"Let's just get it over with so I don't have to dread it all day."

"Okay," she said, starting toward the door. "I—I guess I'll just leave you alone...."

"Oh, no you don't," he said, stopping her. "I can't do this myself. I'd probably cut my lip off. They do want me to keep the lips, don't they?"

Kathryn bit back her grin. "I think so."

"Thank God for that," he mumbled, going to a drawer in his vanity table and pulling out a comb, a pair of scissors and a razor. He dropped them on the table with a clatter and sat down on the swivel chair in front of the mirror. "All right, Kathryn Ellerbee," he said loudly. "Do what they're paying you to do. Transform me."

"Sledge, I can't—"

"Do it before I have time to think. Do it before I decide to storm into Renfroe's office and throw my future in his face."

Kathryn let out a shaky sigh. "All right," she said, realizing that he meant it. "Let me get a towel. Do you have any shaving cream?"

"In the medicine cabinet."

Kathryn got what she needed and went back to Sledge, who was sitting with his head leaning back against his chair. His eyes were vacant and glossed over. The lack of expression contained its own eloquence. Swallowing, she touched the soft whiskers with shaking fingertips as Sledge closed his eyes, bracing himself. A brief memory came back of a cut she'd had on her head as a child, the despair she'd felt over having part of her scalp shaved, the fear of the stitches. The young doctor had talked while he worked, to keep her mind off what he was doing. Perhaps she could do the same for Sledge.

"That picture on the wall," Kathryn began as she lifted some of the whiskers and took the first snip. Sledge gulped in reaction. "The one that says Boston or Bust. How old were you?"

"Not quite twenty."

"Why were you going to Boston?" She snipped again, marveling at how thick the mustache was, how soft it felt to the touch.

"I had a scholarship to attend Harvard."

"Harvard?" He opened his eyes at the surprise in her voice, and she smiled. "Sorry. It's just hard to picture you as an Ivy Leaguer. And on a scholarship, at that."

"But, then, you don't know that much about me."

"No, I don't." Her fingers continued the task. "Was that before or after you went to Vietnam?"

"After."

"Were you a foreign correspondent there?"

"No," he said, closing his eyes again. "Just an innocent kid in a hurry to be a man."

The sullen note in his voice told her she was probing too deeply, so she hushed for a moment as she clipped one pinch of hair at a time, realizing that she was in no hurry to get the task over with.

"You smell good," Sledge rumbled after a moment. "What do you call that scent?"

"Shampoo," she said, ignoring the tingling goose bumps that the breath from his silent chuckle aroused.

"How's it coming?" he asked a few moments later.

"Almost ready for the razor."

His voice took on a dubious edge. "Ever shaved a man before?"

"No, but I shaved a dog once. My little mistake scarred over all right, but he never grew hair there again."

Sledge's eyes flicked open, and he caught her hand, but her amused grin settled his nerves. "Thanks for that bit of reassurance," he said.

"Don't mention it." With one last clip the longer hairs were gone, and only the blade could finish the job. Sledge stretched his lip over his teeth and closed his eyes again as she started to smear foam over his mustache.

"If you cut me, will they let me grow the mustache back to hide the scar?"

"I'm afraid they'd probably opt for plastic surgery, instead."

"Unbelievable," he said. "They tell me I'm perfect for the job, and next thing I know, they want to change everything about me. Why'd they hire me in the first place?"

Kathryn held his face steady with one hand as she made short, smooth strokes with the razor. "They must have seen potential."

"She said skeptically," he muttered.

Kathryn smiled. Sledge opened his eyes on the last stroke and watched her face as she finished. "You have nice hands," he said in a seductive voice. "It was almost worth losing the mustache."

Kathryn pulled back to regard her work. "I thought you were supposed to be mad at me."

"I have a hard time holding grudges against beautiful women," he said. "Tell me. Am I as irresistible without my mustache as I was with it?"

Her lips curled into a faint smile as she picked up the edge of the towel and dried the residual shaving cream from beneath his nose. "You have a very nice mouth," she said softly, tracing her thumb across the smooth skin as if she had a perfect right. "You didn't need the mustache at all."

He brought a finger up to tentatively touch the bare spot as she moved her hand away. "It wasn't a question of need," he said, some of the sparkle dying from his eyes as he looked at himself in the mirror.

"I know," she said. "But in answer to your question, you're attractive with or without your mustache."

"That wasn't the question," he taunted, grinning once again. "I asked if I was still irresistible."

Kathryn leaned against the vanity. "Let's just say that you're as resistible as you ever were."

Velvety laughter rumbled out of Sledge's throat. "Judging by last night," he said, leaning slowly toward her, "I'd say that's a compliment."

"You think a lot of yourself, don't you?" she said as his breath reached her lips.

"Not always," he returned softly. "Last night all I thought about was you."

Kathryn swallowed with great effort, and her smile faded. "I don't think—"

"Good." He took her shaking hands and held them to his pounding chest, his probing, seductive eyes paralyzing her completely. "I never finished showing you my techniques last night."

"Yes, you did," she returned.

"Uh-uh," he argued, moving his hands to her waist and pulling her toward him. "I'm sure I would have remembered."

"I got the general idea." She wanted to push him away, but felt her hands sliding to his shoulders, instead.

"I never deal in generalities," he crooned, and before she knew what had happened, he had pulled her onto his lap and his lips were moving against hers in a primitive language that bypassed the mind and communicated directly to the heart.

CHAPTER THREE

THE MESSAGE WAS CUT SHORT when Kathryn regained her senses and slid her hand up his neck, past his racing pulse, over the smooth texture of shaved skin. Pulling back, she set trembling fingers over his mouth. "Your techniques are—"

"Spellbinding?" he suggested.

"*Refined* was more the word I was looking for," she said, pulling out of his lap to straighten her dress. The heat of desire still coursed through her, making her feel embarrassed. "I can see you've had lots of practice."

"Doing what? Seducing women?"

"Something like that."

Sledge grinned. "So what's so bad about a little seduction?"

"Nothing, under different circumstances," Kathryn said, going back to his closet. "Or between different people. But I'm not in the market for a fling. Besides, I've been hired to do a job, and I find it very difficult to mix professional and personal interests."

"Why?"

She shuffled through his coats, checking the brands of his shirts quickly, as if staying busy could change what had just happened. "Because if I were to allow something personal to happen between us, it would make it impossible for me to give you objective advice, and less likely that you would follow it."

"But you already have let something personal happen between us. Or was that professional? Don't tell me you were simply evaluating another facet of my body language," he teased. "Professional through and through."

Kathryn responded to his gentle humor. "Human through and through."

"Then you do have weaknesses."

"Occasionally."

"Good. Then I'll have to keep watching for them."

Kathryn cleared her throat, but this only made her voice raspier. "Speaking of weaknesses, Sledge," she said, to change the subject. "I see why your producer insisted on a new wardrobe. Your clothes give out conflicting signals. Dysfunctional button cuffs, poor lining, overly aggressive colors."

Sledge stood up and went to the closet to lean against the casing and watch her. "Have I made you nervous?"

"No," she protested—too loudly.

"Then what's all this button-cuff stuff about?"

"It's about my job, Sledge. We have a lot to do today. We have to start from scratch on your wardrobe."

"Wait a minute." Sledge's hands bracketed his hips. "Just because I find you attractive, you've no reason to start insulting my taste in clothes."

Kathryn dropped her head and began to massage her forehead. "You see? There you go. Already you're taking this personally."

"Hell, yes, I'm taking it personally. I haven't run down *your* button cuffs!"

"It's my job, Sledge, and I plan to do it right. Starting with your clothes."

Sledge began to shuffle through his suits as if seeing them from a new perspective. "There is nothing wrong with my clothes. Some of these were expensive."

"But the tone of your wardrobe will set the tone of your interviews. You have a problem with appearing too aggressive and too superior to the people you're interviewing." When she saw his look of disbelief, she threw up her hands. "What difference does it make, anyway? The network is footing the bill."

Sledge smacked the doorjamb of the closet. "It makes a difference when I don't understand why I'm doing it."

"You'll understand when you see yourself in the clothes we buy today. We'll have to start with some semicustom suits, since we'll need them by tomorrow."

Sledge wasn't easily convinced. "If I don't like the things you pick out, I'm not going to wear them."

Kathryn heaved a long sigh. "Sledge, I don't plan to make you dress like a priest. I can see from the things in your closet that you have good taste. It's just wrong for what you do. I promise we'll be able to agree on things."

Gritting his teeth, Sledge started for the door. "All right, then, let's get it over with."

"Not so fast."

Sledge turned around, his head inclined in a "what now?" slant.

"I want you to change clothes. It's better to wear a suit when you shop for one. You'll have to change your shoes, too."

"Are you sure you want to be seen with me in these shabby clothes?"

Kathryn knew the telltale signs of a battered ego. With a note of amusement in her voice, she said, "The tailors know me. They'll understand."

Sledge shrugged in exasperation, then began to pull his shirt off over his head.

"Not here!" Kathryn exclaimed. "In the bathroom!"

His eyes sparkled with teasing innocence. "But this is the dressing room," he insisted.

"Fine," Kathryn said in a huff. "Then I'll wait in the hall. Call me when you're ready." And with that she hurried out the door and into the corridor, accompanied by the sound of his self-satisfied laughter.

ALTHOUGH HE WAS GENERALLY BUSINESSLIKE in his approach to his new wardrobe, Sledge kept his eyes open for what he called Kathryn's "weaknesses." And when he stepped from the store's dressing room in a pair of tight-fitting pants and no shirt, and leaned against the door, he waited for her to gasp in shock or turn several shades of crimson. Kathryn tried hard to disappoint him.

"This may come as a surprise to you, Sledge," she said, trying to keep her professional facade in front of the tailor, "but I've seen a man's bare chest before."

"Not one like this," he assured her.

"You know how it is," she returned, deadpan. "If you've seen one chest, you've seen them all."

"Tell the truth," he prodded. "How would you rate it? On a scale of one to ten."

Though she knew the breadth and definition of his chest, generously covered with dark hair, deserved a ten plus, she merely shrugged. "As chests go, I'd say yours is a seven and a half."

"Seven and a half!" he yelped indignantly. "*This* chest?"

She couldn't give in to him now. "And the pants are too tight."

"They're perfect," he insisted. He turned to the tailor. "I'll take two pair."

"He'll try a bigger size," Kathryn countered, while the confused tailor stood with his measuring tape at the ready.

Sledge flashed a heart-stopping display of teeth that rated at least an eleven. "Tell the truth. You like my chest *and* the fit of my pants."

Kathryn feigned boredom. "For the sake of my galloping pulse, Sledge, go put your clothes back on."

Sledge winked at her before he disappeared into the dressing room, as if he knew her sarcasm was based on fact.

When the fit of his pants was agreed upon and they had decided on several suits that looked as if they had been made for him, Kathryn gave the tailor the network credit card and stacked all the accessories she'd picked out on the counter.

"Will that be all, Miss Ellerbee?" the clerk asked her.

"Yes, I think—"

"Just one more thing," Sledge cut in. He reached over her shoulder and dropped a pair of leopard-skin bikini briefs on the counter. "Since it's on the network," he said, one side of his mouth quirked as he awaited her reaction.

Kathryn picked up the briefs between two fingers, as if the very idea of touching them offended her. "Put them back," she ordered. "The network didn't send me here to buy you risqué underwear."

"Humor me," he whispered. "Only you and I will know what's underneath—and I won't tell if you won't."

Finally deciding that her acquiescence in this token bit of rebellion might appease him through the haircut, which was next on the agenda, Kathryn gave in and bought the briefs. But she threatened herself with bodily harm if she let him know that he'd embarrassed her.

Despite the winks he had given her in the mirror, the conspiratorial grins passed over the fitter's head and the flaunting of his body for her benefit, she sensed deep undertones of hostility from Sledge for her part in changing what he considered his identity. She found herself studying him anew when she thought he wasn't looking, trying to decide if the absence of the mustache made him look better or worse. All the while, she tried to discard the memory of the wonderful feel of the thick, soft bristles, the touch of young stubble on the slant of his jaw.

At the barber's, as she watched his hair being cut, she felt his teasing mood die by degrees with every clip of the scissors. The pensive vulnerability in his eyes struck a discordant note in her heart, and she continually had to shake herself back to her purpose and remind herself of the reason for her strict rules regarding personal involvement with clients.

But it wasn't easy. Even when he was lost in thought, as he was when they took the limousine back to the studio, there was a seductive quality about him that years of training could not help her pinpoint—or ignore. Over and over she found herself studying him, trying to determine whether she liked his short, sophisticated hairstyle better than the longer, disheveled look he had been forced to sacrifice. He sat with his elbow on the armrest, his index finger stroking the skin above his lip.

"You look very nice," she said at last, almost apologetically.

"Mmm," he said.

"Very debonair. Polished."

Sledge gave her an agitated sideward glance. "Just let it rest, will you?"

Kathryn swallowed. "Don't you like the new you?"

"I liked the old me," he said in a wooden voice. He looked over at her again. "Are we about finished? I have a lot of work I need to do this afternoon."

Kathryn had learned long ago when to push and when to step back. "I suppose we've done enough for one day."

"That's the understatement of the decade." He saw the apprehension in her eyes and shrugged. "Oh, I'll get used to it. I wouldn't have done any of these things today if I hadn't wanted this job so badly. But you better believe that as soon as I prove myself to the network execs, I'm going to live and act any damn way I please."

"You know, the changes aren't that radical."

Sledge gave a dry laugh. "Yeah, well, I have the distinct impression that you haven't even scratched the surface—yet."

Kathryn sighed. "Sledge, I'm good at what I do. All of these changes will give you a lot more advantages in your career. You'll see."

But Sledge did not see, and the silence grew stifling between them, until the driver pulled into the studio parking lot where Kathryn's car waited. She got out, racking her brain for some way to make him feel better about his new image before she left. "You really do look nice," she said lamely.

"I'm not used to looking 'nice,'" he said in a poor attempt at humor.

"All right." Kathryn surrendered. "You look devastating. Still."

A twinkle found its way back into his azure eyes. "Mark my words," he said. "In my next contract I'm demanding a mustache clause."

"Sledge," Kathryn said, laughing, "in your next contract you'll probably be able to demand anything you want."

"Yeah. Right," he said obliquely as she walked away.

From her car, she saw the dull glaze settle over his blue eyes again as the limousine pulled into the traffic, saw a finger come up to stroke the bare skin beneath his nose. Had she taken too much from him? she wondered. Had she pushed too far?

It's a job, Kat, she told herself as she turned the key and her car's engine sprang to life. *Just a job.* If only she could see Darryl Sledge as just another client.

KATHRYN'S APARTMENT was a colorful rendition of what she would have been like if her profession had not dictated otherwise. After a hard day of convincing clients how to harness their personal hues—and keeping her own to a minimum in the process—she enjoyed coming home to her sanctuary of conflicting, yet strangely compatible splashes of bright color. It was the one place where she could safely be herself and no one would take advantage of or question her.

But not everyone who came to her apartment liked it. Her sister, Amanda, swore that the wallpaper looked like an artist's poor depiction of a headache, but strangely enough, the sight of it relaxed Kathryn completely. That same sister had made good her threat to "comfort up the place," by leaving her infamous mark in the form of a sofa that seemed devoured by man-eating flowers. Kathryn had kept it with no excuse except that occasionally she enjoyed her sister's symbols of madness.

Madness, Kathryn thought, setting down her purse and notepad on that couch and bringing her index finger to the skin above her lip. Was that what her work with Darryl Sledge was? Madness? Was that what had caused the fluttering in her heart when he'd kissed her today? Or was it madness to have pulled away?

The telephone rang, startling her out of her reverie. The gruff, but satisfied voice of Sledge's producer greeted her.

"Just wanted to tell you what a great job you did on Sledge," Renfroe barked. "He looks fabulous."

"How's he taking it?" she asked with dread. "He wasn't thrilled about letting the mustache go."

"He's great. Listen, I want you here for the taping tomorrow. You'll be able to tell if he makes any wrong moves. Oh, and what do you think about changing his name?" he asked casually. "Don't you think 'Sledge' sounds a little severe?"

Kathryn sank onto her sofa and focused unbelieving eyes on the ceiling. "May I ask you a question?" She kept her voice as calm as she could manage.

"Shoot."

"Why did you hire him to do *InSight*?"

As if the question were absurd, Renfroe grunted. "Because he's brilliant, of course, he has a memory like a Xerox machine, and he knows how to connect details that no one else even sees. There's just no one else like him."

"Then why do you want to make him into someone else?"

Renfroe laughed at that. "Because this is not just a news program. It's show business—entertainment. No ratings, no sponsors. No sponsors, no show. He could be Einstein and still not make it on the air without the right image."

Kathryn had no response. She had heard it all before, had even used the same arguments herself.

"So what do you think about changing his name?"

"I think you should leave it as it is," she said adamantly. "You can only push a person so far."

"We'll think about it," the producer said. "So you'll be here for the taping?"

"I'll be there," Kathryn said without enthusiasm. "And Mr. Renfroe? Don't mention the name change to Sledge yet. All right? His morale isn't at an all-time high."

"No problem," the man said. "If we decide to change it, I'll leave the telling to you, anyhow. Gotta run. See you tomorrow."

For several seconds Kathryn stared in amazement at the phone in her hand before slamming it onto the cradle. During those seconds, she considered ditching her career and becoming a manicurist. She'd always been good with fingernails.

The doorbell rang, and absently biting the inside of her cheek in frustration, she went to answer it. A messenger greeted her with a long, awkward package. "Package for Miss Ellerbee," he announced.

Bewildered, Kathryn took the package, laid it on the floor and dug in her purse for a tip. The first thing her hand touched was the pair of obscene leopard-skin briefs Sledge had bought. Jerking them out of her purse with a look of horror on her face, she turned back to the messenger and gave a nervous laugh. "Practical joke," she explained. She tipped the smirking man quickly and closed the door.

Still holding the bikini briefs, she retrieved the package and examined the brown wrapping for some kind of a card. Finally giving up, she tore into the loose paper. A grimace stole across her face as Darryl Sledge's cardboard likeness grinned back at her.

Propping up the outrageous portrait, she tore off the rest of the paper, this time allowing herself to savor the sight of dark curling chest hair, the dip of his navel, the hard lines of his thighs. Standing back, she shook her head in disbelief at the cocky smile he wore beneath his off-color mustache. Then she glanced once more at the scandalous piece of underwear Sledge had stuffed in her purse. A note was tied around the neck of the cardboard man, and she opened the small envelope and pulled out the message.

A sigh mixed with regret and delight issued from her lips as she read the hand-scrawled note: "In memory of the late Darryl Sledge, who shall one day return to haunt you."

CHAPTER FOUR

"GLASSES!" The word clipped out of Sledge's tight lips instead of a greeting when Kathryn arrived at the studio the next morning, and she braced herself for a verbal lashing. "They want me to wear glasses!"

"I know. Just for this one scene in front of the typewriter." Kathryn surveyed the small set that resembled a busy, cluttered office and set her briefcase down. "I suggested them, to make you look more serious about your work."

He dangled the glasses by one arm and set his hands on his hips. "But there is nothing wrong with my eyes. I don't even need reading glasses."

"That's not the point," Kathryn argued. "The public automatically takes a man more seriously when he wears glasses. And we want to appeal to the public."

"All right," Sledge said, holding his hands up in mock surrender, his irritation obvious. "Then we'll move on to my next gripe. I don't work on a typewriter. I use a computer."

"We aren't trying to mimic reality here, Sledge. How many times do I have to tell you that we're just trying to—"

"Appeal to the public," he mocked in an unflattering voice. "For what? Pity...laughter?"

Kathryn pushed at the riotous curls spilling over her forehead. "Do you want your pilot to be a success, or not? If you want to do a second show, you'd better get it through your head now that we have to use every gimmick we can to make people watch the first show. We can't worry about the real you when we're trying to win a viewing audience."

Sledge jammed his hands in his pants pockets and looked back at the props. "So that's it?" he lamented, bringing troubled blue eyes back to her maddeningly unwavering expression. "The decision has been made to give the viewers some idiotic idea about who I really am, and I have to go along with it?"

"You got it." Kathryn reached up to straighten the collar of his pale blue shirt, open at the neck and rolled up at the sleeves—the costume representing a man too busy at work to worry about cuffs and ties.

Sledge tried to fight the grin pushing away his scowl. "Would you mind not pulling at my clothes while I'm mad at you? It's a little distracting."

Kathryn disengaged her hand and raised sparkling black eyes back to his. "Sorry. Did you have another complaint?"

"I'll come up with something," he said, a grudging curve to his lips. "You look good in purple."

The remark took Kathryn by surprise, and she examined her polished-cotton dress. "Thank you."

"You're welcome." His smile grew broader as if he knew he was finding his way back on top, and Kathryn decided they'd better return to the subject.

"Look, Sledge," she began, as if their argument had never been detoured. "The viewers don't know you yet. We've got to fling your integrity and your dedication in their faces in triple doses just to draw them in."

Sledge stiffened, but his anger did not resurface. "I still don't know why the network didn't hire a little bald man with bad eyes to do this show. So far I don't seem to have any assets."

Kathryn tried to call up a contorted Renfroe expression to her face, and she schooled her voice to imitate the producer's gravel one. "He's brilliant, has a mind like a Xerox machine, connects details no one else sees. There's no one else like him."

Sledge worked on a sulk, though a small grin broke through again, like sunshine refusing to be snuffed by clouds. Setting his hand on her shoulder, he ran his thumb across the purple fabric of her collar. "If only I looked more like Truman Capote."

Kathryn laughed. "Don't worry. If the first show's a success, I'm going to suggest having that cardboard poster of you duplicated for advertising."

He tugged on her collar, his hand warm against her neck. "Duplicated? Don't want to part with yours, huh?"

Narrowing her eyes, Kathryn stepped back and flicked her hair over her shoulder. "I've been meaning to talk to you about that. I intend to give the poster back to you as soon as I can find a discreet way to get it out of my apartment," she said. "And speaking of discretion, I want to talk to you about the underwear you stuffed into my purse."

Sledge's eyes danced with devilment as he feigned innocence, but before he could answer, Renfroe spotted Kathryn and hollered across the studio, "What do you think, Kathryn? How does he look?"

"Like a distracted, nearsighted man who'd wear exotic underwear," Sledge mumbled, shoving his glasses on.

Kathryn ignored Sledge and waited for the producer to approach. "Like a man who won't rest until he gets the story done," she said, her eyes silently telling Sledge to wipe the sleazy grin from his face.

Shrugging, Sledge went to the set, letting the aura of glaring lights envelop him. He sat down at the typewriter, looked around for a switch to turn it on and emitted a loud moan. "A manual typewriter? Give me a break! Am I not supposed to be aware of modern technology?"

Renfroe grumbled and sauntered toward the set. "It's a symbol, Sledge. One that people can identify with."

"But I can't type on this thing," he argued.

"No one's going to see what you're typing," Renfroe said. "Just act."

"But I'm not an actor!"

Renfroe waved the retort aside as irrelevant. "Do you have your lines down?"

"Yeah," Sledge said, shifting gears from one gripe to another. "I have them. But I don't mention my name anywhere. Shouldn't I—"

"We'll dub that in after we get the various shots of you at work," Renfroe cut in smoothly. "Don't worry about it."

Kathryn stepped up beside Renfroe as the taping started, her perceptive dark eyes entrapping the producer. "You're leaving his name out?"

"Yeah," Renfroe whispered. "Just until we decide what to do about changing it."

"You're the producer," she returned, more to remind herself than him. "But I have to say again that I think changing his name would be a colossal mistake."

"We'll keep your opinion in mind," the man said absently as Sledge began to type.

Pushing down her irritation, Kathryn watched the mischievous gleam in Sledge's eyes being replaced by diligent absorption in his work. He was completely believable in the hurried way he tore the paper from the typewriter and handed it to someone off camera. She listened as he faced the lens and the home audience with perfect preoccupation and uttered his lines about always being on top of and up-to-date on every development in his stories, and how watching his show could keep the viewers just as informed.

Impressive, Kathryn thought, stepping closer. He was good at what he did, mainly because, no matter what props and gimmicks they gave him, his strong personality penetrated the layers of falsity and commanded the viewers' undivided attention. Her changes were simply window dressing to guarantee that the viewers' first glimpse of Sledge was a pleasant one. She only wished his producer could see her task as such a simple one.

After several takes to achieve different camera angles and accommodate a minor technical difficulty that developed, Sledge was allowed to step out of the lights and prepare for the next spot. In this one he was to be fully dressed in coat and tie, and he gladly left the eyeglasses in his dressing room. This scene promised to be easier, for it was being taped to look like impromptu pieces of conversations containing his views about the public's "right to know." In this scene he had the opportunity to reveal his personality, his humanity, his charisma and his world outlook, which pleased him to no end—until he realized the amount of makeup that was being painted on his face.

"From one extreme to the other," he muttered almost inaudibly as he sat rigidly in the makeup chair, while Kathryn looked on.

"Trust us," she cajoled. "These scenes will be great."

"Right," he said caustically. "Do I get to sing in the next one?"

"No, Sledge," she said, trying not to grin. "No singing."

"But we want them to think I'm well-rounded, don't we?"

"Yes," she agreed. "But we don't want them turning down the volume. We'll save your singing debut for one of the later shows."

The set for the next spot resembled a plush living room, and Sledge was seated on a love seat. When told to relax, he spanned one arm across the back and crossed his legs.

"Too bold. Too superior," Kathryn asserted, shaking her head. "How about if you rest your chin on your hand?" Moving him into position, she felt the tension settling into his muscles. She stepped back and assessed the new pose that contradicted the hardening of his eyes. "Try it," she told the crew.

The camera started to roll, but the director stopped the scene in midsentence. "Too stiff. Too coiled," he said, turning to Kathryn.

"How about resting your elbow on the arm of the love seat?" she suggested, checking the misalignment of his shoulders.

The camera started to roll again, but Renfroe halted the scene before it got very far. "Too relaxed. Too sloppy," he said.

Kathryn frowned and went back to Sledge. "How about uncrossing your legs?" she said. "And maybe straightening your body a bit."

Sledge acquiesced, and the camera rolled again, only to be stopped by the director a moment later. "Too serious. Too deadpan."

Kathryn noted the angry color creeping up Sledge's neck. "How about smiling a little, Sledge?"

The slash across his face broadened in a poor imitation of a smile, and the muscles in his jaw clenched visibly.

"No, a little more," she prodded. "Give us a little flash of teeth."

Sledge's nostrils flared, but he did as he was told. The camera rolled again, only to be stopped after he began his lines.

"Too little feeling. Too—"

"What the hell is this?" Sledge bellowed, grabbing his tie by the knot and yanking it off. Slinging it across the set, he stood up. "A conspiracy? Is it some form of slow torture? An endurance test?" He unbuttoned his shirt collar and dragged off his coat.

"Sledge, we aren't finished. Put your coat back on," Renfroe said in a placating tone that only served to make Sledge angrier.

"What for? So I can sit down and let you people play Simon Says with me again? What the hell do you need me for? Why don't you just get a look-alike robot and program it to do what you want it to? Then I can get some real work done and everybody'll be happy."

Kathryn stepped forward. "I know it's hot under the lights, Sledge," she said, carefully keeping condescension out of her voice. "But this is part of the show whether you like it or not. Please, just sit down and let us work it out. Put your jacket and tie back on."

Sledge met her eyes, silently proclaiming a stalemate. Lifting his chin, he began to unbutton his shirt defiantly, tore out of it and slung it onto the love seat, his thick brows arched in a what-do-you-want-to-make-of-it challenge. Standing bare-chested before the cameras and crew, he scowled at Kathryn. "If I'd wanted to be a toothpaste model I'd have stayed in Dallas and signed up with Lou Ellen's Modeling Agency, making a living grinning instead of thinking." He strode off the set, his fast gait forcing those in his way to step back.

"But Sledge, we aren't finished," Renfroe shouted.

"Maybe *you* aren't," Sledge called back. "But *I* am!"

And to Kathryn's utter dismay, no one tried to stop him.

"Well, don't just stand there. Go after him and get him back here!" Renfroe ordered Kathryn, as if the demand were a perfectly natural one.

"Me?" she asked. "Why me?"

"Because you're supposed to be the expert at handling people."

Kathryn stood her ground stubbornly. "You don't throw a lion tamer into a cage with enraged lions just because he's an expert!"

"Well, we don't have time to wait until Sledge is calmer. Everything's set and ready to go. Go use that sweet-talking female charm of yours to soothe his ego, but get him back in here immediately. Time is money!"

"It sure is!" Kathryn agreed. "And I don't spend my professional time practicing feminine wiles."

"Just do whatever it takes, for Pete's sake," the producer snapped, making her dislike him even more than she had previously. "If you can't handle him you sure won't be able to handle the exercise-show host who's next on your list. You might as well practice on Sledge's ego, because that guy's is a whopper."

Kathryn wondered what the market was like for bomb defusers these days. The work would be more predictable and infinitely less dangerous. Grinding her molars, she gathered Sledge's discarded clothes from the set and marched out of the studio.

Kathryn found him in his dressing room moments later. He opened the door for her and eyed the clothes in her arms. "What did you do? Draw the short straw?"

"What?" she asked, not attempting to hide her annoyance at his behavior.

"Is that how they got you to come in here and take on my temper?"

Kathryn pushed her way past him into the dressing room and threw his clothes down on his couch. "No. They mentioned the fact that they'd hired me to do a job, and whether I like it or not, this little problem falls under that heading."

Sledge dropped onto the sofa, his eyes as chilling as they had been under the hot lights. "Looks like I'm ruining your day."

Kathryn stalked to the bar and pulled out a polished glass. "You aren't exactly making it easy."

"Well, if it's any satisfaction, you're ruining mine, too."

He watched as she checked the liquor bottles on hand, chose the Scotch and poured some into a glass, ignoring the liquid sloshing up the sides. "That bad, huh?"

"That bad," she confessed, taking the glass to him. "This is for you. If I had my tranquilizer gun with me, I'd shoot you. Since I don't, I've decided my best bet is to tame you with alcohol before trying to get you back out there."

That seemed to amuse him, and he took a drink and let the liquid burn out his temper to a degree. "Well, you're on the right track. You'll definitely have to get me drunk to make me into whatever it is you people expect me to be out there." He held the glass up, studying the liquid. "Specs and a primitive typewriter one minute, movie star makeup and a glittering smile the next. Terrific. You're sure they don't want me to sing?"

Kathryn rested her forehead in the palm of her hand, willing away the headache that was beginning to take hold. "We're simply trying to show different facets of Darryl Sledge," she explained, for what seemed like the thousandth time. "To make the audience feel they know you."

"Know *me*? Or some clone that you and Renfroe came up with?"

Kathryn made a mental note to look into bomb squad jobs more seriously when she got home.

Sledge sipped some Scotch and set the glass down. "I think the problem, Kathryn Ellerbee, is that none of you experts know yet who you want me to be. So you swing back and forth between extremes. But see, I know who I am. If you'd let me be myself, you wouldn't have to work so hard. And just maybe I could give the audience what they want."

"And just maybe," Kathryn responded quietly, mocking his tone, "you'd turn them off completely, and they'd watch the sitcom on another network instead of your show. Just maybe the experts know what they're doing."

Sledge plunked his elbows on his knees and wearily rubbed his eyes. "I'm a reporter. I interview people. And I'm good at it. And interviewing has nothing to do with sex appeal or the clothes a man wears or how big he smiles. It has to do with insatiable curiosity, instinct and listening. When I did that documentary on the terrorists holding the Americans hostage in Beirut, it wasn't me the viewers saw. It was the story. Nobody cared about my clothes or whether I wore glasses. They cared about what I had to share with them. That's what got me this job in the first place. Not some cocka-mamy image I worked up."

He got up and went to a drawer in his vanity table, pulled out a pack of cigarettes and shook one out. Kathryn watched him set it between his lips. "I didn't know you smoked," she ventured.

He swung around as if she'd just told him his feet were too big. "I don't. I quit a few months ago, so don't you dare tell me that I have to quit for my damned image, or I might have to start back again. Got it?"

She wet her lips and tried not to smile.

With the unlit cigarette hanging from his lips, he plopped himself back onto the sofa and glared at her. "When I get mad, I want to smoke. I don't light it. I just hold it. The taste makes me feel better. All right?"

"All right." She looked at the floor and tried to redirect her thoughts. "Look, there's a lot at stake here." She leveled her gaze to his. "Too much to gamble on. These promo spots need to be calculated, strategic and provoking. They're promoting you more than the show. It has nothing to do with your talent as a reporter. It's business—and you know it. If this job means anything to you, you'll put your clothes back on and get back in there."

"I should have been a newspaper journalist," Sledge mumbled.

"Yes, well," Kathryn said, "if you keep this fight up, that might be where you wind up. And I have a feeling that your heart's in television broadcasting, or you wouldn't be here."

Sledge clasped his hands together as a rest for his chin and issued a long fathomless sigh. "You know, when I was a kid I used to watch Walter Cronkite and hang on his every word, thinking how wise he was—how he knew everything. I thought then that if I could be anything I wanted, I'd be a newsman like him. I'd have integrity, grit, perception." He took the cigarette out of his mouth and picked up his drink, rolling the glass between his palms. "So I signed up to fight in a war to give me a more defined world view. And I struggled for top grades at Harvard to sharpen my intelligence. And I went back home to start working my way up until I could someday have a network job. Only to find that perception and education and experience aren't enough. Wonder if Cronkite ever had to put up with this stuff?"

"Bet on it." His spontaneous revelation softened Kathryn's expression, robbing her of some of her antagonism. "And someday there'll be children who'll see you and want to follow in your footsteps. They won't remember Walter Cronkite, but they'll know Darryl Sledge. First we've got to make sure they see your show."

Sledge locked into her gaze while her argument thrashed around in his head. He looked at the cigarette, breathed in its scent and stuck it back in his mouth. "In other words," he said, "I owe it to future generations to go out there and smile like I'm pushing deodorant."

"I couldn't have put it better myself," she said.

He seemed to consider the possibility for a moment as he stared into his drink. Then, with a mammoth sigh, he set down the glass.

"Can't let down all those poor kids milling around without role models, now can I?"

"It would simply be a crime," she said.

Casting her a dubious look, he grabbed his shirt, shrugged it on and buttoned it. Standing up, he pulled on his suit coat and slipped the tie around his neck. Then he picked up the glass and leaned over Kathryn. "Here," he said, handing the Scotch to her. "You probably need this more than I do."

Kathryn looked down at the liquid. "I don't drink when I'm working," she said, "although I strongly considered breaking that rule today. Let's just say I can relate to your need of a cigarette."

Sledge smiled and took the cigarette from his mouth. Then he leaned on the arms of her chair and brought his face close to hers. "Let's make a pact," he said in a voice that was more seductive than professional. "I'll trust you to know what you're doing, if you trust me to know what I'm doing."

Kathryn nodded, realizing that it would take more effort to trust him than it would to fight him. But she tried to take heart. If her career as an image consultant failed because of her work with Sledge, she could always fall back on fingernails or explosives.

KATHRYN KICKED OFF HER SHOES as soon as she was inside her apartment and collapsed on the sofa, reveling in the glorious silence. Once she had gotten Sledge back in front of the camera things had gone smoothly, but no one could have mistaken Sledge's cooperation for enjoyment. When the camera wasn't rolling, he was as tense as a bowstring. And so was she, waiting for his blue eyes to lance her, as if she, alone, were responsible for the injustice of his profession.

She yawned and told her muscles to let go their rigid guard, since in her apartment there was no chance of a subtle, sensual attack or a temper blowing up with the force of a nuclear weapon.

The flashing red light on her answering machine beckoned her, but she tried to ignore it. She counted the flashes before it rested momentarily. One. Two. Three. What was Amanda's dilemma today? she wondered wearily. Was she trying to decide between fuchsia and chartreuse fingernail polish? Had she met a nice guru who had asked her to meditate with him? There was no predicting Amanda's messages, but Kathryn could always expect them to be entertaining. Her sister used the answering machine like therapy. She would call with a question, answer it herself, then call back again. Amanda admitted it was a lot cheaper than a psychiatrist—and it never rejected her.

Kathryn stretched out toward the telephone table and punched the button for message retrieval, bracing herself. Her sister's hurried voice said, "Kat, what does a thirty-one-year-old woman wear to a Bruce Springsteen concert? Oh, and how do you feel about mohawks?"

Kathryn cringed. A mohawk? If she knew her impetuous sister, she had probably already ruined her hair. The tone sounded, and her sister was on again.

"Forget the mohawk. I just found out Springsteen isn't punk. Is it okay to wear black boots in June, or do I have to wait until after Labor Day?"

Kathryn shook her head. Since when did Amanda worry about seasons in the clothes she wore? The tone sounded again, and Amanda's third message began.

"Forget the boots. I've decided to go billowy. Can I wear that pair of pants you bought, the ones I said looked like deflated balloons? I've decided I like them, after all."

Kathryn closed her eyes as the dial tone signaled the end of the message. The machine began to rewind. Should she rush to call her sister back? she wondered, or had Amanda already changed her mind and decided to go neon? Since she had divorced her husband, a playboy who had stifled and neglected her for years, Amanda had been on a journey of self-discovery, and Kathryn had a hunch she'd found more to herself than she'd bargained for.

The doorbell rang, and Kathryn grinned, knowing before she answered it that it would be her sister.

"Forget the pants," Amanda said, bursting in. "They'll make me look fat. How about that white skirt you have with the frayed edges? By the way, do you like my hair?"

Kathryn frowned and examined the kinky black strands that boxed at Amanda's chin. She looked as if a triangle had been set over her head! She reached out to touch her sister's hair, then drew back when she felt the wiry stuff. "Just one question, Amanda," she said, wincing. "Why?"

"Why not?" Amanda bopped into the kitchen to pour herself a drink. Kathryn followed, unable to keep a mournful look from her face. Amanda's hair had been so soft, so lustrous, so...

"Oh, stop." Amanda said, laughing. "You don't really think my hair would do this, do you? It's just a wig."

Kathryn sank against the doorway in relief. Then she *had* set a triangle over her head. "Amanda, I don't know how many more of your self-improvements I can take."

"Then you don't like it?" Amanda's wide black eyes danced in spite of her sister's disapproval, and she gave a one-sided grin.

"Not particularly. But I didn't like the hot pink streaks last week, or the Tina Turner teased look the week before. It didn't faze you then, did it?"

"Not a smidgen," her sister said, sampling her drink on her way to Kathryn's bedroom.

Kathryn stayed in the kitchen to pour herself a drink. "Amanda, no one says 'smidgen' anymore," she called out, though she felt quite sure her sister didn't care. Suddenly a blood-curdling scream shook the apartment, and Kathryn set down her glass and bolted to her bedroom.

Amanda had found the life-size image of Darryl Sledge.

Kathryn stifled her laughter because she'd heard that it wasn't polite to laugh at people who had just brushed with cardiac arrest. Her sister had fallen back onto the bed and was clutching her chest, trying to catch her breath. Kathryn pulled the poster out of her closet so that Amanda could have a better look. "Want one for yourself?" she asked. "Every red-blooded American woman should have one."

Amanda closed her eyes. "Good thing I've kept up my aerobics. A weaker heart would have bought it just then. Where in the world did you get that?"

Kathryn sat next to her sister on the bed and studied the Sledge poster with her. "He's my latest client at the network," she explained. "He's hosting a news program. I'm supposed to change his image, but he's resisting all the way. He sent me this so I wouldn't forget the original version.''

Amanda, whose vital functions were returning to normal, let her eyes roam over Sledge's magnificent body. "Excuse me a minute while I drool,'' she said. "Hosting his own show, huh? Pretty important. Is he by any chance lonely?''

Kathryn smiled. "Does he look lonely?''

Amanda shook her head and sighed. "And you want to change him?''

"It's my job,'' she said evasively. She stood up and stuffed Darryl Sledge back into her closet. "Now what did you want to borrow?''

"How about him?'' Amanda ventured, pulling her cigarette case out of her purse.

"I don't believe he loans himself out.'' Kathryn found the skirt with the fashionably frayed hem and held it up to her sister.

"Or maybe you don't want to share him. . . .''

"Share him? Amanda, don't get the wrong idea. I'm not interested in getting involved with clients.''

Her older sister lit her cigarette and peered at the poster of Darryl Sledge. "Then, my dear little sister, you must be a fool.''

"Not yet,'' she said, treating herself to another look at the poster herself. But in spite of her resolve not to be victimized by the man, she realized that she was fast learning the way to becoming a fool. And it was a harder road to avoid than she'd thought.

CHAPTER FIVE

SEVERAL DAYS PASSED before Kathryn was able to work a session into Sledge's hectic schedule, but when she did, she found him waiting for her in his dressing room with more than a little enthusiasm. His crystalline eyes sparkled with exuberance when he let her in, and she found the turnabout distressing.

"The whole afternoon to kill," he exclaimed as she set down her briefcase, opened it and got out her list of "Sledge Flaws."

"Not 'to kill,'" she said, turning back to him. He wore a pair of beige cords and a brown, loosely meshed pullover, pushed up at the sleeves to reveal corded, sinewy forearms. Stifling her curiosity about how he kept his deep tan when he always seemed to be working, she tried to look efficient. "We have a lot of work to do. I hope we can get everything done that I have planned for today."

"How about a Coke first?" he asked, sauntering toward his bar and pulling out two glasses.

"Sure." She watched as he bent over the small refrigerator.

He pulled out two cans, popped the tops and poured. "So what does an image consultant do when her subject is as busy as I've been lately?"

Kathryn shrugged and examined her notes. "Work on her other clients."

"You mean there are others?" he asked, crestfallen.

She smirked. "You might find it interesting to know that I'm working on a soap opera actor for this network right now who needs to be less polished. It's convenient. I can just swap some of your traits and go from there. I hope you don't mind. I gave him some of your lines to use on women—to enhance his playboy image."

Sledge's eyes glistened as he brought her the drink. "You liked those lines, did you?"

She took the glass he offered. "They were original. But somehow they didn't seem as effective coming from him."

In fact, she thought ruefully, nothing she'd done for Brad Miller had seemed very effective. When she'd discovered that he had nothing but peach fuzz for stubble, her idea to make him grow a mustache had been discarded. She'd bought him clothes like the ones Sledge had, but on Brad they didn't have the same effect. And when she'd suggested that he try blue contact lenses, only to find that they made his pale face seem even paler, she'd suggested that he get a tan. He was at that very moment basking hopefully under a Bahamian sun.

Sledge's brows cropped upward in amusement as she sat down. "You have to mean those lines to make them sound effective. They don't work for just anyone. Besides, I've had years of practice."

"Yes, well," she said with a sigh. "I guess there's no substitute for practice. Even I can't work miracles, I suppose."

Sledge gave a sly grin and leaned over her, his breath teasing her lips. "Poor guy hasn't got a chance with smooth operators like me stalking around, huh?"

Kathryn stiffened and leaned back. "Even smooth operators hit rough spots now and then," she warned. "Which brings us to why I'm here."

Sledge considered the list she held. "So what steps are you going to take to make me into a Milquetoast? Let's see," he said, reading, "my accent, my walk, the way I move my eyes, the places I go at night..." His eyes lost some of their luster. "Lord, woman. You forgot to add the position I sleep in and which shoe I put on first!"

Kathryn scooted away from him, trying to cover up the rest of the list. "It isn't as bad as it looks, Sledge. I'll try to be gentle."

He sat down opposite her on the couch, every bit the playboy warming up to his subject, though his blue eyes held a hint of worry. "So what's the matter with the way I talk?" he drawled in an exaggerated accent that rivaled Rhett Butler's.

"It's a little heavy for national television," she said. "Too Texas."

"Too Texas," he repeated. "I'll keep that in mind. I do a great Massachusetts. Or would you prefer Connecticut?"

"Just try neutral, hot shot." She set down her glass, pulled some tapes out of her briefcase and dropped them on the couch between them. "I want you to listen to these tapes and practice until you've lost your accent. If you haven't lost it by the end of next week, the network will send you to a speech therapist. And I'm not kidding."

Sledge rubbed his face with a callused hand, making it red. "They could always dub in a voice. Use my face and someone else's voice. It wouldn't be any more absurd than any of the other stuff."

Kathryn focused on the ceiling. "Sledge, this stuff is not absurd. The network's complaints seem to be valid ones. You should concentrate on the benefits to be gained from these changes."

He was quiet for a moment. "You're right. There is a positive side, isn't there?" He leaned toward her, his eyelids lowering seductively. "So whose voice is on the tapes?"

"Mine," she said.

"Great." His voice deepened in pitch. "I'll take it to bed with me every night. You can whisper me to sleep."

"There's no whispering on these tapes," she assured him, making a valiant effort to ignore the way he seemed to be getting closer to her. "Just a lot of repetition."

As if he didn't hear, he reached out to capture a stray strand of her hair and swept it back from her face. Her heart bolted at the brush of his fingers against the crest of her cheek. She stared at her notes, trying to get her thoughts back on track. "Now let's see. What's next?"

"You always smell so good." He inched a little closer and inhaled deeply.

"Sledge, please," she said, but she knew that the protest meant a small victory to him.

"Anything," he offered.

"We have work to do. There isn't time for chitchat."

He chuckled close to her ear. "Chitchat? Is that what we're having?"

"Your walk," she said firmly. "We have to talk about your walk."

He smiled and rested his jaw on his hand. "What about my walk? I've been told it's sexy. And speaking of sexy walks, do you know what caught my attention the night I saw you coming into the bar?"

"I couldn't care less," she said, swallowing. "Sledge, you're making our work very difficult today. Please, just—"

"What's the matter?" he asked in a voice that she would have sworn was serious if she hadn't known better. "Do you lose your train of thought when I sit so close? If I'm flustering you, I'll move."

He was smart. She had to give him that. He somehow knew that she would no more admit to being flustered by his nearness than she would admit to having really liked his mustache. "I'm just fine," she bit out.

At that his eyes seemed to darken from the inside out, and she had to force herself to keep her purpose at the forefront of her mind. "And whether you like it or not," she finished, "we are going to discuss your walk."

He tried to suppress a yawn. "Okay, Sarge. Go ahead. Tell me about my walk."

Kathryn got her breathing back in rhythm and considered using tact, but decided it was too much trouble and would be misinterpreted, anyway. "It's somewhere between a strut and a swagger," she said bluntly. "You'll have to tone it down a little."

His eyes widened with delight. "A strut and a swagger? Me?" He considered her assessment for a minute. "I can't picture what you mean."

"You know," she said, determined to wipe the smugness off his face. "A cross between a pimp and a pirate."

Sledge frowned thoughtfully and stroked his chin. "Should I try limping? Pimps don't limp, do they? Some pirates do, I suppose, but you can't have everything."

Kathryn was amazed at the way he remained undaunted. Did he take none of this seriously?

"Don't like that idea, huh? Okay, I'll think of something else."

"Can I ask you something?" she said, anger shaking her voice.

"Is it personal?"

"Not particularly."

"Oh." The space between his brows furrowed. "Well, I guess you can ask, anyway."

"Do you think this is funny? Do you think the network hired me to lighten up your days a little?"

He shrugged with incorrigible indifference. "They've been known to waste money on sillier things."

"And you think that my job is one of those silly things?"

"Hey, I didn't say that."

Kathryn sprang up from the sofa and confronted him. "Get up, Sledge!"

Sledge stood up reluctantly, honestly trying to hide his amusement. "Should I roll up my sleeves? Are we about to slug it out?"

As much as Kathryn wanted to answer his unflappable grin, she wouldn't allow herself to. "Walk across this room," she ordered. "And put a little more Cronkite and a lot less Travolta into it."

"Yes, ma'am." He walked in front of her, then pivoted when he reached the wall and held out his arms as if he'd finally gotten it right.

"Wrong," she said.

"Well, I'm sorry." Sledge looked serious at last, possibly exasperated. "And I know it shows a terrible lack of observation on my part, but I honestly haven't ever noticed how Walter Cronkite walks!"

"He walks with dignity!" she said. "As if he doesn't care how he looks from behind."

"And you think *I* do?" Sledge struck a stubborn stance. "You think it's my fault women like the way I walk? You think I do it consciously?"

Kathryn was getting angrier by the moment. "I don't think half as many women notice your walk as you care to think, Sledge."

"*You* did," he pointed out, equally angry.

Kathryn compressed her lips and tried to keep from screaming out in frustration. Only Sledge could take what most men would have considered an insult and twist it into a compliment about his sensuality. And only Sledge would be so dead sure it was nothing else. "I have never worked with anyone so stubborn!"

"Neither have I!" he flung back.

"You're giving me a headache," she snapped, going back to the couch and jerking up her clipboard.

"And you're giving me a pain in the neck," he volleyed.

She started toward the door, but he stopped her. "Where are you going?"

"Anywhere!" she said, swinging back toward him. "I can't do anything with you today. You're bullheaded, Sledge. There are other clients who appreciate the help I can give them."

"I'm sure there are," he said. "Clients who need help to begin with. *I* don't happen to."

"I'll see you tomorrow morning, Sledge," she said. "I don't intend to waste any more time butting heads with you. I don't have to remind you what's at stake here."

"No, but you will," he yelled after her as she stormed out the door. "As many times as it takes for me to hop to like all those other little idiots you try to revamp."

"I don't revamp idiots, Sledge!" she shouted, and stopped dead in her tracks. "I simply try to make people fit into jobs they probably shouldn't have in the first place! And if I can't make them fit, the network can always find others who will!"

Sledge went to the door and leaned into the hall. "Oh, go mold a clone, Kathryn Ellerbee."

"You know," she said in an explosive whisper, "I could see myself becoming violent with you, Sledge. You bring out the worst in people!"

"And you bring out the best?" he scoffed. "How much better the world must be since you came along. If it weren't for you, everyone might walk wrong and wear mustaches and talk in accents. You let something like that get out of hand and you never know where it might lead."

Kathryn shook her head helplessly. "I can't even communicate with you. If you aren't trying to conquer me with your little one-liners, you're badgering me with sarcasm."

"They call it self-defense," he said. "In case it hasn't occurred to you, I don't like being fake."

"They call it *ego*," she said. "You're not afraid of being fake—you're afraid of admitting you aren't perfect."

"Look who thinks she's perfect. You don't see me going around trying to change people."

"I'm trying to *help* people, and if you weren't such a—"

"Don't call me names," he cut in. "I haven't called you any names."

"If you weren't such a mule-headed—"

"I warned you not to call me names," he said with a sigh, and as if he had no other choice, he jerked her back into his dressing room and closed the door, his expression suddenly mendaciously calm.

"I'm not afraid of you," she spluttered.

"Well, you should be, sweetheart," he bit out, stepping frighteningly close to her. "Because I'm afraid of you. I haven't had my emotions beaten around like this since I was in the second grade and Freda Lynn Anderson called me a 'wiar.'"

Kathryn felt her anger dissipating by degrees as the warmth of his body seemed to press into hers. "She called you a what?"

"She meant *liar*, but she couldn't pronounce her *l*'s. I got so mad I wanted to hit her, until I realized she had a bigger fist than I did. So I did the only thing I knew that would truly put her in her place."

And before Kathryn could object, he had taken her shoulders and was kissing her with all the passion that had been reared by their explosive words. The surprise tactic shook her, melted her, paralyzed her, and she groped for reason, knowing that by conceding this victory to him she would lose some of herself.

So she summoned the small amount of strength she still had and told herself a little bit would have to go a long way. But as she tore out of his embrace, she realized that the principle worked with passion, as well. It only took a small taste of Sledge for her to know she wanted more.

"Freda Lynn Anderson slapped me," Sledge whispered, his face mirroring her surprise. "But she never called me names again."

Kathryn groped for some comeback that would put him in his place, but her whirling thoughts refused to comply. So, telling herself she wouldn't give him the satisfaction of physical response, she turned and fled from the room.

KATHRYN STOOD IN THE ELEVATOR the next day and shook the rain from her long curls and her skirt, as if brushing off the wetness were as easy as putting Darryl Sledge out of her mind. No, she told herself. She would not think about him now. She had wasted an entire sleepless night over him, and she would not be distracted from her work today. Her skin glistened with dampness, and she cursed herself for having forgotten her umbrella that morning. The elevator doors opened at the twentieth floor, and she picked up her wet briefcase and started down the hall, trying to pretend that facing Sledge after yesterday's ambush would be as easy as stripping him of his mustache had been.

Sledge's office door was closed, so she knocked tentatively. There was a lull in the strained conversation inside, and she heard Sledge call, "Come in."

A pervading sense of danger consumed her at the sight of Sledge hunched over his desk, shoulders raised, an unlit cigarette in his mouth. Renfroe sat across from him, fidgeting with his tie.

"We were just talking about you," Sledge said forebodingly, taking the cigarette out of his mouth between scissored fingers.

"Should I leave?" Kathryn asked, setting down her briefcase. The rain pattered against the window at Sledge's back, making abstract patterns on the pane, framing him in stormy splendor. But the light of the warm office drew attention to his face and massive shoulders, and her heart skipped a beat at his virility and harnessed power.

"Absolutely not," Sledge said. "Since our discussion has to do with how you're going to spend this evening, I think you should stay."

Renfroe ignored Sledge's undisguised hostility and turned to Kathryn. "Forget your umbrella?"

"Afraid so," Kathryn said, glancing warily at Sledge as she again dusted the wetness off her full green skirt and sat down. She felt Sledge's gaze sweep over the cascade of her hair, then down to her breasts, where the thin, damp fabric clung. Stiffening her back, as if to restore the dignity that the rain had taken away, she inclined her head toward Renfroe. "So what's this about the way I'm going to spend my evening?"

"The party," he said, patting his shirt pocket for a breath mint.

"Oh, yes," Kathryn said. She had almost forgotten about the party the network employees were obligated to attend. After all, it wasn't every day that the network won a major lawsuit brought on by a congressman who'd felt slandered. The president insisted everyone celebrate in accordance. "Tonight, isn't it? Don't worry, I'll be there."

Renfroe resorted to his pants pockets in his absentminded search for a candy. "I want you to go with Sledge."

Sledge bristled and sat up in his chair, thumping his cigarette filter against his desk. "As if I can't find my own date."

"Do *you* have any objections?" Renfroe asked Kathryn.

"Obviously he does!" The admission hurt.

"No problem here," Sledge clipped. "I do what I'm told these days."

Kathryn huffed out an irritated breath. "You really know how to flatter a woman's ego, don't you?"

"Who cares about ego when you're dealing with public image?" he asked. "It's just one of the many sacrifices for the cause."

"The cause?" Kathryn's cheeks began to sting, and yet the frost in his eyes sent a shiver snaking down her spine. "You consider a night out with me a sacrifice?"

He lifted his brows as if he were innocent of having offended her. "I'm just trying to cooperate. Hey, I realize I need a baby-sitter to tell me how to act at the party. Don't want any public blunders, do I? Your being there will ensure my acting like a perfect gentleman.''

Kathryn ground her teeth and mentally counted to ten. It was Renfroe's fault, she realized. If the idiot had used more tact in making his request, Sledge wouldn't be playing the martyr now. "Why don't you take someone else, Sledge?" she offered.

"I thought about it," Sledge said, still thumping the tip of his cigarette. "But I don't know anyone else who can see quite as much wrong with me as you can. Someone else might let me make an absolute fool out of myself."

"Well," said Renfroe, bolting up, as if he'd just seen two happy people come together on a deal, "since that's taken care of, I'll get back to work."

Kathryn and Sledge sat locked in each other's gaze as Renfroe slipped out of the room and closed the door. Then Sledge jammed the cigarette back into his mouth.

"I don't know when I've been so swept off my feet." She crossed her arms. "Tell me. Did you rehearse the way you asked me, or does this brand of charm just come to you naturally?"

Sledge leaned forward again and jerked the cigarette out of his mouth. "I resent the hell out of being told who I'm to be seen with in public. I've had pretty good luck getting companions in my life so far."

"I'm sure you have," she grated. "And so have I. This wasn't my idea, you know."

"Wasn't it? Haven't all of the little surprises I've been subjected to been your ideas?"

Kathryn stood up. "Some of them were," she admitted. "It's my job to make changes. But if you think I'd use my position to make you take me to a stupid party, you're more demented than I thought." She grabbed her briefcase, prepared to leave. "Take anyone you please to the party tonight, Sledge. I already have plans to go with someone else."

"Renfroe won't like it."

"I don't care what he likes!" she shouted. "Nowhere in my contract does it say that I have to date you. Believe it or not, I don't like having my companions chosen for me, either. You're sitting there so smug, thinking that you've got the short end of the stick. Why, you've never even considered that you might be the last person on earth I'd want to wind up with at a party."

Sledge was completely taken aback, and Kathryn seized the opportunity to start toward the door. "I'll come back tomorrow, and we'll view some of your problem segments together. I think I'll just work at home for the rest of today." She reached for the doorknob and started to turn it. Sledge was behind her in an instant, pushing the door shut. "Wait a minute," he said, trapping her, a hand on either side of her. "I didn't mean to offend you."

"Don't flatter yourself," she said, glaring up into his face. "I'm not some sixteen-year-old kid who just had her feelings hurt."

"Then why are you trying to run out of here again?"

"Because I'm mad, that's why."

"At me or Renfroe?"

"At you. Renfroe's stupidity is to be expected. Yours continues to amaze me."

Sledge didn't answer right away, but the hint of a smile glistened in his eyes. "Stupidity, huh?" he asked finally.

For a moment she thought he might consider that name calling and give her the Freda Lynn Anderson treatment again. This time she'd bite his tongue, she decided. "Stupidity," she repeated.

Suddenly his proximity became threatening. She felt her heart dancing beyond its normal rhythm as his face loomed closer to hers and his breath reached her face. "Come to the party with me, Kathryn Ellerbee," he urged her.

Kathryn emitted a high-pitched laugh. "You've got to be kidding."

"I'm not. I want to take you."

"Sledge, I don't need to be appeased just so you can handle your producer. I can take care of Renfroe, if you can't."

"I don't care about Renfroe. I want you to come to the party with me. You said I could take anyone I pleased."

Kathryn closed her eyes. Was he always this unpredictable? "Did we, or did we not just have an explosive argument about the fact that you desperately didn't want me as your date?"

"That's not what the fight was about," he said. "It was about my being told who my date would be." He leaned closer until his forehead almost touched hers. "See, I was going to ask you, anyway."

Now what was he up to? Kathryn stared with disbelief into his riveting eyes. "You really think I'm dumb, don't you?"

"No," he said, his grin confident, as if he could see and was greatly satisfied with the effect his mere presence had on her. "I think you're beautiful. I think you stimulate me mentally and physically to the point of insanity. And I'll die if I can't take you to the party tonight. I just wanted it to be our idea, not Renfroe's. For pleasure's sake, not for the good of the network. He made me so angry that I would almost have gone alone to spite him."

"And what changed your mind?" she asked without conviction.

"The sight of you—wet and mad," he teased, plucking the collar of her wet blouse. "I hope it rains again tonight."

Kathryn felt herself blush like an adolescent misfit in the presence of the quarterback. "I told you I'm going with someone else."

"Cancel," he coaxed. "I'll leave my sarcasm at home, and I'll be the perfect gentleman. I'll even wear the clothes you bought me. Right down to the underwear."

Kathryn pursed her lips to stop from grinning. "But I still have the underwear."

"Then I'll wait until I get to your place to put it on."

She whispered a laugh and shook her head. "You're impossible."

"To stay mad at?" he asked. And when she didn't answer he knew he'd won. "Then you'll come?"

She heaved a long sigh. "I really did promise another client I'd go with him," she said regretfully. "I can't cancel."

He straightened, all hope of victory gone. "That actor?"

"Yes," she said.

"I can't believe it. You'd actually choose some two-bit soap star over me?"

She smiled. "Yes."

"You're going to make me go to the party alone?"

"Maybe Freda Lynn Anderson is available."

Sledge winced. "You're a real heartbreaker, Kathryn Ellerbee. Making me pull out my little black book and everything."

Kathryn reached for the door again. "You'll survive."

"You can't go yet," he said. "I thought you were going to teach me how to walk or something."

This time Kathryn turned back into the room of her own free will, and she realized that it wasn't in her destiny to figure Darryl Sledge out—not all at once, anyway.

CHAPTER SIX

THE DOORBELL RANG before Kathryn was dressed for the party, and she cursed Brad Miller. Lesson number forty-two, she thought. Never pick a girl up a half-hour early. Darryl Sledge would have been at least five minutes late. But Brad was her date tonight, and she would have to enjoy it, even if he did expect her to literally tell him every move to make. On the soap opera his character was handsome, rugged, virile, and used layers of makeup. And as long as he had a director to tell him what to do, Brad was fine. Real life was another thing.

Tying the belt of her robe around her waist, Kathryn opened the door. "Brad, you're a half—"

But it was Amanda who stood before her, clad in a tight dress of sparkling green sequins, the lids of her eyes painted in fluorescent stripes, her hair done up in a pretzel-style knot on one side of her head.

"Where are you going in that?" Kathryn asked.

"Oh, this old thing?" Amanda shrugged. "Nowhere. I don't have any plans tonight. So I just threw this on and thought I'd drop by to see what you're wearing out with Brad Miller." She said the name reverently, and Kathryn saw right through her sister's act.

"If you wanted to meet him, Amanda, all you had to do was say so when you called earlier to interrogate me about my plans for tonight."

"I want to meet him." Amanda parroted with excitement. "He's *so* sexy on television. What's he like in person?"

"Different," Kathryn hedged, slipping out of her robe. She handed Amanda the periwinkle gown she planned to wear that night. "Here, make yourself useful and see if you can find a way to get into this thing. I couldn't find a zipper anywhere."

"I have one like it. You undo the straps," Amanda explained, "but it's a little tricky." She began to work the straps loose, but her attention was still on Brad, and Kathryn's interest in him. "He doesn't seem like your type, though."

"Right," Kathryn agreed, taking the bait. "More like your type." Amanda handed her sister the dress, and she started to squirm into it. "Hey, I have an idea," Kathryn said, as if the idea had just occurred to her. "Since you're dressed up and everything, why don't you come with us?"

"Me? Tonight? Oh, I couldn't," Amanda said, grinning from ear to ear.

Kathryn shrugged and let her sister refasten the strap. "Suit yourself," she said. "If you don't want to."

"Well, if it would help you . . ." Amanda left the sentence hanging.

"Oh, it would, Amanda." Kathryn deadpanned. "It really would."

The two women began to laugh, and Kathryn wondered if poor Brad Miller was really ready for the likes of Amanda. At least Kathryn would be too worried about him to waste much thought on Darryl Sledge.

Who would he bring to the party? she wondered. Had he tapped the resources in his little black book? She tried to picture his address book, and imagined a couple of volumes the size of a Sears catalog. He'd probably show up with a blonde on each arm just to spite her.

The doorbell rang, shaking her out of her meandering thoughts, and Amanda shouted, "I'll get it!"

Kathryn closed her eyes and pitied the man on the other side of the door.

Brad's producer had once told Kathryn that when God made Brad Miller he used a worn-out mold. Therefore the only trait he was well endowed with was dullness. It wasn't his fault. But she had found it more and more difficult to forgive him lately for being bland. For that reason Kathryn was grateful for her sister's overenthusiastic greeting when she answered the door.

"Jonathon Rugby in the flesh," Amanda exclaimed, referring to Brad's television character. "Come in here, you big hunk."

It took all her energy, but Kathryn suppressed her grin. It was always best not to encourage Amanda. "Hello, Brad," Kathryn said. "You look nice."

Brad stood stiffly in the room, eyeing Amanda the way one would a psychopathic lioness. "Thanks."

"But it isn't quite right for you somehow," Amanda said bluntly, standing back to look at his black tux and the combed-to-perfection style of his blond hair. "The tie has to go, don't you agree, Kat? I'm her sister," she directed at Brad, "but she never remembers to introduce me. What about the tie, Kat?"

Kathryn gave a helpless have-at-it gesture, and her sister went to work on Brad. When the bow in his tie was undone, he gasped, "It took me forty-five minutes to tie that."

Amanda slipped off the tie and threw it over her shoulder. "Well, that should have told you something right there. Anything that takes that much trouble couldn't be right. Besides, Jonathon Rugby would never wear a tie."

"But I'm supposed..." His voice trailed off when Amanda began unbuttoning his shirt.

"Look at that chest," she said in an awestruck voice.

Brad looked at the door, as if measuring his chances of escape. He cleared his throat nervously.

"Now isn't that better?" Amanda asked seductively. "You're so much freer to be yourself."

One side of Brad's thin lips cocked upward as he looked reluctantly down at his admirer. "Yeah, you're—you're right. As long as Kathryn thinks it's okay."

Kathryn tried to imagine how Sledge would have dressed tonight if Renfroe hadn't given him strict orders to dress formally. He would have certainly gone tieless. "Amanda's right," she said. "That is better."

"One more thing," Amanda said, sliding her hands along his shoulders. "The hair needs to be more tousled. Sort of—" she slid her fingers into his hair and did a finger massage to mess it up "—like this. What do you think, Kat?"

Kathryn stared up at the job her sister had done. "Well, it does make him look more relaxed."

"It's lethal," her sister cut in, punctuating her pronouncement with a mock growl. "You'll have to fight me off all night. That is, if you don't mind my coming along. I've been wanting to meet you ever since Kat started working for the network," she purred.

"My sister has the subtlety of an earthquake, Brad," Kathryn said. "But she means everything she says."

Confidence was beginning to surface in Brad. "I thought I'd lucked out getting one beautiful woman to come with me to the party," he said. "And now to have two? I'd love it."

He jutted out both arms, one for each woman, and Kathryn suppressed a yawn. It was going to be a long evening.

THE ELEVATOR that would take them up to the Park Avenue penthouse was almost full of clashing fashions and scents of perfumes and colognes that were never meant to mingle. Kathryn blinked, trying to stop her eyes from misting. She glanced up at the blond man beside her and saw that Brad seemed genuinely flattered by Amanda's blatant attention. He kept his hand possessively around Kathryn's waist, though, as if to assure her that she was still his date.

"Hold the elevator," a deep voice called as the doors started to close, and Kathryn's heart lurched when Darryl Sledge stepped between them, his presence causing the elevator doors to spring back open for him.

He squeezed in and leaned against the wall next to Kathryn, the rich lines of his black tuxedo coat drawing her eyes down the length of him, then back up to the crisp white shirt he wore. A light floral scent of herbs and forest drifted toward her, wiping out the battling fragrances she had smelled before, and the special male signature of Darryl Sledge assaulted her senses.

She held her breath as he made a sweeping assessment of her, his eyes sparkling with approval. Then he leaned down, his mouth shiveringly close to her ear. "Little lady, you'd have blown Venus right out of Olympia, looking like that," he whispered.

She groped for some flip return that would make her seem unaffected by his magnetism, but just then Brad Miller cleared his throat and pulled her more possessively close to him. Sledge's eyes darted to the man, and Kathryn couldn't help but notice Brad's reaction to virility personified. Brad squinted, for he had not yet got used to his new contact lenses, and he looked decidedly uncomfortable.

"New contacts, huh?" Sledge asked amicably.

Brad tried to stop squinting, and squared his shoulders. "Yeah," he admitted grudgingly. "You wear them?"

"Me? No, these babies are the real things."

Brad decided to focus on the numbers flashing over the elevator doors. Sledge's amused eyes collided with Kathryn's, but she would not be drawn in.

The elevator doors opened to reveal the elaborate foyer of the network president's suite, and the partiers spilled out. Sledge fell into step beside Kathryn, and Amanda dragged Brad to the bar. "I see what you mean about some of your clients needing more help than others," Sledge said, nudging Kathryn.

Kathryn lifted her chin and met his eyes directly. "Don't you have a date you can badger?"

Sledge shrugged. "I hate making complicated decisions. So I came alone."

"Tell the truth, Sledge," Kathryn teased, her glistening eyes reflecting unaccountable delight. "You couldn't get a date, right?" Even as she spoke, she knew the idea was about as likely as Michael Jackson's forgetting how to moonwalk.

Sledge looked down at her, a disarming grin getting comfortable on his face. "The truth is that I wanted to be free to administer first aid when you started dying of boredom."

"Are you referring to my date?"

Sledge winked. "Don't worry. If it gets too bad we'll just slip out. I have a limo waiting down—"

"*We'll* just slip out?" she asked. "I didn't come here with you and I'm not leaving with you. Is this your incredible version of first aid?"

Sledge just grinned more broadly and ran a finger down the jeweled strap at the shoulder of her dress. "It's one of the first steps," he drawled.

Kathryn's smile vanished, and she stepped back. "You never learn, do you, Sledge? You're amazing."

"Thanks," he said, undaunted.

"If you'll excuse me, I do have a date."

"It's a mercy date if I ever saw one," Sledge mumbled as she started away.

Bristling, Kathryn turned back to him. "If you think about it, you'll realize that I chose one mercy date over another. Brad's producer takes an interest in his dates, too."

Suddenly Sledge's eyes blanched to the pale color of frost. "I'm not going to let that little remark ruin my evening," he said in a deceptively mild voice. "If you change your mind about slipping away with me, just call. The offer still stands—until someone else diverts my attention. That should take about ten seconds."

And then he left her standing alone, feeling as if she were an abandoned date at a party of strangers.

But the people were not strangers. She was surrounded by the people she worked with, many of whom she saw daily. Yet the only person who seemed to matter in the noisy room was Darryl Sledge, and right now he was walking into a circle of starlets, who perked up immediately at his attention.

"Amanda said you liked white wine," Brad commented, barely penetrating the fragile bubble she felt inflating around her. He handed her the glass as she wrenched her eyes away from Sledge. Brad slid his hand into one of his pockets and began to jangle his keys with nerve-racking intensity. "So what do we do first?"

"Well, we try to relax, for one thing," she said. Brad, she noticed, had unbuttoned his shirt farther since his arrival at the party. Ordinarily the small lapse in formal conformity would have given a more rugged devil-may-care look to the subject. But in Brad's case it only made him look as if he'd forgotten an important part of his apparel. A shock of hair hung over his forehead, and unable to stand the sight another moment, Kathryn reached up to set it back in place.

Brad seemed to enjoy the personal attention. He squinted down at her, in a way that must have been intended as seductive, and she shivered. "Why don't you go dance with Amanda?" she suggested kindly. "She's really a lot of fun."

He obediently scanned the room for her sister, and Kathryn used the moment to search out Darryl Sledge. Although he seemed engrossed in deep conversation with a sultry-eyed redhead whom Kathryn recognized as Shelly Somebody from network news, occasionally his eyes met Kathryn's over his companion's head. The woman, Kathryn judged, was waging a full-scale attack as she leaned toward Sledge, her false eyelashes batting out invitations too hot even for Morse code. When he offered the woman that Sledge-smooth smile that boiled Kathryn's heart at fifty paces, she was certain he had forgotten her completely.

"How about if I dance with you, instead?" Brad asked, nudging her with his elbow.

Kathryn spoke without thinking. "Brad, it's not good for your image to stick to one woman all evening. The network wants you to play the field. Flirt a little. Love 'em and leave 'em." She couldn't believe the words coming out of her own mouth.

Brad, however, was delighted. "Well, it sounds great, but I honestly don't know where to begin."

"That's why we brought Amanda. If anyone can teach you how to flirt, she can. Just loosen up a little and she'll have you looking like a wild man in no time. But Brad, she's more than just a fan. She likes you a lot."

Brad snickered. "Okay. I'll go look for her, then. And you'll be all right?"

Kathryn tried to be patient. "If I run into trouble, I promise to scream."

She watched him push through the crowd, and strained her imagination to see him as a sex symbol— but it wouldn't stretch that far. He tried to walk in beat to the music, but his timing was a bit off.

What was the matter with her? she asked herself. She had never had such a poor success rate with two clients at the same time. None of her efforts had worked on either Brad or Sledge. She knew what the problem was with Sledge. He was too stubborn, too sure that his image was stable, too set on proving he was right. And with Brad, she suspected she'd been a bit distracted. She kept trying to make him into a Darryl Sledge, and that was like trying to turn Phyllis Diller into Brooke Shields. Amanda's lessons in flirting would probably do more for Brad in one night than Kathryn had done in two weeks.

She scanned the gaily dressed guests crammed into the posh penthouse until she found Amanda in her sparkling green gown. Her stomach plummeted when she saw Amanda brandishing a foot-long cigarette holder and talking to Sledge.

Quickly bottoming her drink and setting it on a table, Kathryn bolted through the crowd. "Amanda, I've been looking for you."

"Why didn't you introduce me to your sister in the elevator?" Sledge's tone of voice was irritatingly cool.

Amanda answered before Kathryn could. "Because we've really already met. Or at least I've met you. Kat, have you seen Brad?"

"Yes," Kathryn began. "He's looking—"

"We've met?" Sledge cut in. "Where? I have a good memory and I don't—"

"In Kat's bedroom," Amanda explained quickly. "Now about Brad. Where—?"

"Her *bedroom*?" Sledge sliced through her question.

If faces could glow in neon, Kathryn's did. "Brad's at the bar. Go dance with him!" she sputtered furiously at her sister.

"Wait a minute!" Sledge said. "You met me in her bedroom?"

"The stand-up poster," Amanda explained distractedly, waving him off with her cigarette. Then she flounced off. Kathryn tried to follow, but Sledge grabbed her arm and hauled her back to him, his eyes glittering.

"You keep my poster in your bedroom?"

"Closet," she bit out. "Bedroom closet. It's the only closet I have, and your poster was too big to throw away."

Sledge sailed past her excuses. "You keep my poster in your bedroom. I like that."

"Don't let your ego run away with you, Sledge. It doesn't mean a thing. Now if you'll excuse me, I'll leave you to Shelley What's-her-name."

"You know," he said, as if he hadn't heard a word, "that might just make me forgive you for your nasty little remark earlier. I might just rescue you, after all."

"I told you, I already have a date."

Sledge found the green flash of her sister's dress in the crowd and saw Brad and Amanda dancing. "Looks like he's being well cared for. Better than he ever imagined. By the way," Sledge said, a frown furrowing his brow, "how come he got to come without a tie and I had to dress like some kind of butler?"

Kathryn grabbed a glass of wine from a passing tray and took a gulp. "Because you are supposed to look like Walter Cronkite, and he's supposed to look like Brooke Shields." She caught herself and moaned. "I mean he's supposed to look like—"

"Darryl Sledge?"

Kathryn took another gulp of wine and began to see the humor and hopelessness of the situation. "He's supposed to look like the character he plays on television."

"Not easy, huh?" Sledge asked, beaming down at her and setting a hand on her shoulder.

"I've had a bad week, Sledge," she admitted with a surrendering smile. "I have one client who won't take my advice no matter what I do, and another who tries very hard but just can't pull it off."

"I'm taking your advice," Sledge argued. "Didn't I dress like a gentleman tonight? I combed my hair and everything. And I've only given one lady an enticing invitation, though she still insists she won't leave her date." He ran his finger across the fastening of her dress again, melting her nerve endings. "And I've been listening to your tapes over and over," he murmured in a voice that made her heart rate accelerate. "I don't know what it's done for my accent, but it's done wonders for my imagination."

"Sledge!"

"Really," he drawled. "You have a very sensuous voice."

Kathryn looked down at her drink, and told herself that if she did somehow leave this party with him, she'd better lay some ground rules about what he could expect. Otherwise she might find her heart without a choice.

"Sledge—"

"See, you can't stop murmuring my name. It drives me crazy. Come home with me, Kathryn Ellerbee."

"I can't."

"You won't," he corrected.

"Right," she agreed. "I won't. I told you before that I don't get involved with my clients."

"But you came here with one. The least you could do is not show favoritism. I deserve equal time, don't I?"

Kathryn looked up to see Brad coming toward her again. She couldn't remember when she had let a client's need for her aggravate her so, but, then, the circumstances tonight were unusual.

"Do you want to dance now, Kathryn?" Brad asked.

Sledge set his arm possessively across Kathryn's shoulder and leaned toward Brad, his voice conspiratorially low. "Hey, pal, as one of her clients to another, let me give you a little advice. The best thing you can do to enhance your playboy image is to come to the party with one date and leave with another. Nobody'll miss it."

"But I don't want—"

"For the network, Brad. They've been good to you."

"But Kathryn—"

"Don't worry about her. I'll see that she gets home all right. I think if I were you I'd start paying more attention to her sister. You should see how that woman looks at you."

Kathryn was speechless as she listened to the exchange, and she wondered if Sledge had ever considered selling used cars.

Brad blushed and glanced toward Amanda, who waved boldly. "She does seem to like me," he admitted, looking questioningly at Kathryn, who groped for some sort of answer.

"She—she really does. She couldn't wait to meet you. Don't worry about me. I'll be fine. Being seen with Amanda might enhance your love-'em-and-leave-'em image." What was she saying? Was she paving the way for her to go home with Sledge? Was she crazy?

Sledge's feathery touch along her dress strap sent a warm shiver down her spine. Yes, she was crazy, she told herself. But if anyone was going home with Sledge, it was not going to be Shelly Whoever.

"Well, all right," Brad said, eyes sparkling. "If you think it's the right thing to do."

"Go ahead," Kathryn urged. She watched as Brad sauntered toward Amanda, and then she turned to Sledge, wagging a finger in his grinning face. "This means absolutely nothing. I'm doing this because Amanda does like Brad, and I think she'll do more for him than I can. This does not mean that I'm inviting you for a roll in the hay. You may take me home, and that's all. Got it?"

Sledge made a show of nodding sheepishly. "Got it. Ready to go?"

"Now?"

"Why not? I hate these kinds of parties. All that's really required is that we put in an appearance, anyway. I've congratulated our illustrious president for getting us off the hook. I've complimented the hostess.

And I've even had my picture taken a couple of times. What else is there to do?" As if in answer, his hand slid seductively up her shoulder, stopping at the wild pulse point on her neck.

"Nothing, I guess."

He stroked her neck with his thumb and began to guide her toward the door. "Come on. Let's leave before Miller loses his nerve."

He ushered her into the elevator, and Kathryn had the nagging feeling that if she had any sense at all, *she* would be the one to lose her nerve.

"Wait. We're going up!" she exclaimed as the elevator began to move.

"Smart lady." Sledge's indolent blue gaze warmed her.

"But I thought—"

He silenced her with his thumb, and his fingers cupped her chin and tilted her face upward. "Trust me," he whispered.

"Trust you," she repeated dubiously. She tried to relax, for she feared that any crack in her feelings would give away too many of her thrashing emotions.

The elevator doors parted quietly, and a warm gust of night air swept in. Sledge's grin possessed a seductive quality that she could not help answering. "After you, lovely lady," he said, gesturing toward the roof of the building.

Kathryn held back. "Is this your way of getting revenge? Are you going to throw me over so I'll stop trying to change you?"

Sledge chuckled. "Do I look like a vengeful man?"

"You look like a man with something up his sleeve," she said.

His grin broached wider across his face, and the sparkle in his eyes outshone the cloud-veiled stars. "What I have up my sleeve has nothing to do with vengeance," he said, leaning against the open elevator doors. "I simply want to share one of the most beautiful sights in the city with you."

Reluctantly Kathryn accepted his hand and stepped out of the elevator. Around her, Manhattan was a million tiny lights shining heavenward, a stark, but pleasant contrast to the inky blackness above them. She drank in the sight around her, then turned back to Sledge. "How did a Texas boy find a sight like this?" she wondered aloud.

Sledge leaned back against a concrete riser. "The network biggies wined and dined me before I signed my contract. They brought me up here to impress me."

"And did they?"

"Impress me?" He took a deep breath and looked around, and she marveled at the luminous blue of his eyes even in the darkness. "Hell, I've seen beauty before," he continued. "And I've seen big cities. But there was something about the activity here, the hustle and bustle, the power and intelligence packed in each one of those buildings, on each one of those floors, in every room. I can't think of any place else in the world with so much energy. So many answers, so many secrets. How could a journalist not want to live here?"

Kathryn let her gaze linger on him for a moment. His head was cocked in a way that invited and promised, and yet he did not make a move. "I've heard New York referred to in a lot of different ways," she said at last, "but never like that."

A breeze whispered through his hair, ruffling it in a way that made her want to run her fingers through it, but she kept her distance.

She swallowed when he lifted his chin and pulled his tie out of its bow, then opened the first three buttons of his shirt. A shiver coursed through her at the warmth and sensuality he exuded, and she wondered if the effect was deliberate.

"Cold?" His voice was barely audible over the thick sounds of city night.

She nodded and turned back to the skyline. He would suggest they go home now, she thought ruefully. And the evening would be over soon. Gone would be the music of the wind and distant sirens below; gone would be the peaceful lights that spoke of a million separate lives; gone would be the bond that she felt with Sledge.

But Sledge made no move to leave. "Come here," he said in a husky voice, and he reached out to pull her into the vee of his legs.

Kathryn wasn't certain why she didn't resist when he turned her away from him, wrapped his arms around her waist and set his chin on her shoulder. Perhaps it was because the gesture seemed so innocent, so devoid of intention, and yet so intimate.

"Do you know how beautiful you look under the stars with the wind dancing in your hair?" he whispered.

She didn't answer, for she only wondered if he knew how compelling he was with Manhattan as his backdrop, the smell of night and impending rain mixing with the magnetic scent of his cologne.

"Tell me about Kathryn Ellerbee," he said softly. "Tell me about the woman who studies people and changes them, leaving a trail of broken hearts everywhere she goes."

Kathryn shook her head, but she didn't dare meet his eyes, for the proximity of their lips would allow no retreat. "I don't know who told you that."

"No one had to tell me. All I know is that the first time I saw your eyes across a crowded barroom, I knew I was going down for the count. Didn't matter, though, because I wanted you."

She fidgeted nervously, but his arms tightened around her. "Sledge, I don't—"

"Shhh," he soothed. "We're not talking about that right now. We're talking about you. About who Kathryn Ellerbee really is."

"You know who I am."

"But who were you? A high school cheerleader? Homecoming queen? Did you have a different date every night, or did you date just the quarterback? You probably edited the yearbook. And the school paper. And you constantly had to go around behind your sister getting her out of trouble. But you were never in trouble, because you played it safe."

She smiled at the accuracy of his impromptu history of her life. "You think you're pretty smart, don't you?" She turned her head for a response, and realized what a grave mistake she'd made, for his eyes seemed even bluer than ever, more devastating, more breathtaking.

"Well, am I wrong?" His voice was grainy, peppered with emotion.

"What about you?" she asked, hedging. "Quarterback who dated the homecoming queen and head cheerleader officially, but everyone else unofficially? Voted most handsome every year, most likely to succeed, wittiest—"

"You think I'm handsome?" he cut in.

She looked away. "Even you think you're handsome, Sledge. That's no secret."

He laughed, and her heart rate escalated. "It doesn't matter. Good looks are a dime a dozen. It's my brains and my personality that attract you to me. I know, because that's what attracts me to you. The way you think. The way you act."

She swallowed, and her uneasiness returned. "And who says I'm attracted to you?"

"No one says," he whispered, his lips magically close to hers. "No one has to say."

He kissed her in soft supplication and slowly turned her in his arms. Her hands lit on his shoulders like butterflies ready to flee at the slightest movement. He parted her lips beneath his, and the taste of his velvet tongue sent her heart careering. One of his hands moved along her face in satin strokes that made her feel soft and special, somehow precious.

A raindrop fell between them, lighting on Kathryn's nose, and then another plunked onto Sledge's eyelash. "It's raining, Kathy," he whispered against her lips. "Looks like I got my wish." And then he kissed her again.

The raindrops came closer together, no longer a force to be ignored, and Sledge pulled back with a ragged sigh. "Your dress, while I love the way it clings to you, will be ruined," he whispered. "I've got to get you inside."

Mutely she acquiesced, as he led her back toward the elevator. The sudden splash of light broke the spell, giving Kathryn time to reprimand herself for her feelings. "Maybe I should get a taxi home," she said quietly. "Maybe this isn't such a good idea."

Sledge slid his hand up her arm and caressed her neck. "I'm taking you home," he said with a note of finality. "You think I could just put you in a taxi and wave goodbye?"

"But . . . it's a mistake. Things shouldn't go any further."

"They'll only go as far as you want them to," he promised, but she found no comfort in his words, for it was herself she feared.

"You can take me home," she said finally, "but I don't want you coming in. I mean it—no pressure."

"No pressure," he agreed solemnly.

Sledge had arranged for wine in the limousine, and he poured her a glass when they were on their way, sipping from it first. Then he flicked on the stereo and feigned innocence at his obvious attempt at seduction when the tender strains of a Bach violin concerto filled the air. The private compartment separated by glass from the driver, the rainy darkness and the lit signs whisking by combined to give Kathryn a feeling of unreality, leaving her with nothing to cling to except the glass in her hand and the little voice in her head crying out, *beware!*

"You're pretty when you're pensive," he said, touching her chin and drawing her face toward him.

Kathryn smiled as if she'd heard that line before, and he took one of her hands, fondled it in his.

"You're pretty when you smile," he added.

Her eyes widened as he brought her hand to his mouth, kissed each knuckle, his soft lips making her part her own unconsciously.

"You're pretty when you're helpless," he whispered, pressing her hand against his face.

Taking a controlling breath, she pulled her shaking hand out of his and wrapped it tightly around her wineglass. "Not helpless, Sledge," she said quietly. "Not yet."

"Then soon," he predicted.

And Kathryn felt a fluttering sense of uneasiness that his warning rang too true.

CHAPTER SEVEN

THE LIMOUSINE STOPPED in front of her apartment building, and Kathryn got her purse and held up a restraining hand to stop Sledge from following her. "I told you I don't think you should come up," she said.

"Come on, Kathy. You can handle me."

Kathryn's cheeks flushed. "I just think it's a bad idea."

Sledge pointed out the window. "But the rain—it'll ruin your dress. At least let me walk you up. I'm the man with the umbrella."

Kathryn wondered for an insane moment if he'd made some arrangement with the powers of the universe tonight to take part in his thorough seduction. But the orchestration didn't matter so much, she admitted to herself finally. She wasn't quite ready to leave him.

"All right," she said with resignation. "But just to the door."

Sledge got out and opened the umbrella, tucked Kathryn under his arm and pulled her along at a trot, into the building and up the stairs. He took the key from Kathryn's hand when she got it out, and opened the door to her apartment, stepping in before she could stop him.

Sledge closed the door behind them, and Kathryn reached for the light switch. "I *said*, just to the door."

Sledge caught her hands before she could flick on the light, and pulled them around his waist. His palms slid smoothly, maddeningly, up her back. "You didn't say which side of the door," he whispered, and before she could issue her heart a retreating order, his lips claimed hers in a kiss that stripped her soul bare.

Kathryn's hands molded his chest, measuring the desire hammering from his heart. Her fingers slid higher, touched the rough beginnings of stubble on his chin, then brushed through his mink-soft hair.

He worked at freeing the bobby pins from her hair to let the coiled curls fall around her shoulders, then brushed his fingers through the fullness. She reveled in his taste—sweet, like wine—and breathed in his masculine scent. But when his roving hands stopped their drugging seduction to release the strap of her evening dress, she caught her breath and broke the kiss, murmuring, "Stop."

He didn't seem to hear. Instead his lips moved to the outer corners of her mouth, and his hands moved to undo the other strap.

"Don't!" she said more loudly.

He pressed his forehead against hers. "Why?"

Holding her dress in place, she slipped out of his arms and turned on a lamp. His smoldering eyes took in the disheveled state of her hair and the unveiled shoulder. "I've told you why." She tried to hook the strap back in place but failed.

Sighing with resignation, he took the strap and deftly hooked it up for her before moving away to allow her the space she seemed to need.

"I see you've had lots of experience getting into dresses like mine," she said with a defiant lift of her chin.

"Either that, or I've spent the entire evening trying to figure that strap out."

Kathryn wilted against the door. If only he would come back with something predictable, she thought, something that could be pigeonholed based on her studies, something to convince her that he was absolutely wrong for her. But he wasn't predictable. He was sly, and he was shrewd—and he was still waiting to make another move. "Well, you managed to satisfy your curiosity. You can leave now."

"Nothing about tonight has been satisfying," he whispered, taking a step toward her. "And undoing that strap only piqued my curiosity more."

Kathryn tried to fight her bewildering emotions with flippancy. "Come on, Sledge. If you've undressed one, you've undressed them all. Besides, I'm not your type."

"How do you know what my type is?" He took another intimidating step closer to her.

She took two steps back toward the couch.

"I didn't do all my research for *Gestures* for nothing. You like them freer than I am, looser. You like women without inhibitions, and I have lots of them. And you like them classically beautiful, which I obviously am not."

Sledge inclined his head and laughed under his breath. He took another step toward her. Again she stepped back, this time skirting the sofa. "What have you got?" he asked quietly. "A chart with personality types and backgrounds? Can you just cross-check to see what type of woman I could go mad over? Have you already looked it up?"

The back of Kathryn's calf collided with the sofa, and she stopped. "Of course not. But I have more perception into human nature than many people do."

"If that's the kind of woman you think I want, then your perception is seriously flawed." With a couple of lazy steps, he caught up to her again.

Realizing their motions were beginning to resemble a slow-motion dance, Kathryn rooted her feet to the carpet and vowed not to move again.

"What is it about me that you like, Sledge?" she asked. "Is it the challenge, the chase? Is it the satisfaction of trying to best the person who dared to tell you there are ways of improving yourself?"

"You've given this a lot of thought, haven't you?" he asked, an unabashed sparkle in his eye. He stepped toward her again.

"Yes," she said. "I've been through this before. Patients fall in love with their psychiatrists because they depend on them for emotional support. It's called transference. My clients fall in lust with me because they want to prove they're not as bad as I've told them they are. You think I've taken a bit of your manhood from you, and you want to prove that you still have lots in reserve.''

The luster in Sledge's eyes died. "You must feel pretty good about yourself, knowing you have such a positive effect on people.''

Kathryn recognized his sarcasm and crossed her arms defensively.

"Thing is,'' he went on, "if you wanted my manhood, all you had to do was ask for it." He took yet another step toward her, so close that her folded arms were sandwiched between their bodies. "You know, I've learned a few things from working with you. And I read your book last night. Photographic memory, remember?''

Kathryn pushed her hair back. The heat emanating from him seemed suddenly overwhelming, and she sank onto the sofa. He followed. "All right, Sledge,'' she said, crossing her legs and trying to look composed, even bored with his banter. "What kind of things do you think you've learned?''

"That when a woman keeps pushing her hair back the way you do, she's preening for her man.''

Kathryn set her hand back in her lap. "I'm not preening. It's hot in here and I want my hair out of my face.''

"Right,'' he said with a wink. "And the way you led me to the couch while making it look like it was my idea . . .''

"What? I—''

"And the way your shoe is hanging from your toes, bobbing when you swing your leg. No man needs a book on body language to read a signal like that."

"What signal?" Kathryn cried. "That my shoes are too big?"

"And your pupils are the size of dimes. In your book you said that pupils dilate when people see something they like," he went on in a raspy whisper. "Explain that one away."

"The lights are dim in here. Besides—" her voice dropped to a whisper as his face moved closer to hers "—your pupils are enlarged, too."

"I don't doubt it," he whispered. "And I don't deny the reason, either."

When his lips caught hers again, she held back, not parting her lips. But his tongue painted desire over them, outlining them, and the velvety wetness prompted her to allow him entrance. Her hand came up to his chest as their mouths made subtle advances and withdrawals, testing and tasting before joining completely.

She felt her rationale melting like ice beneath summer sun, felt her muscles relaxing as she gave in to the emotions swaying her. On a wave of frustration she realized that he wasn't touching her with his hands. Trembling with restraint, she shushed the admonishing voice inside her and told herself that a kiss without his touch was like a voice without his face, a tease without substance.

Carefully she made the first move. She touched his face, molded the shape of his jaw and traced the lines of his eyebrows. Then she felt him pulling her down with him, back against the sofa. Her breasts crushed the hard lines of his chest, while their legs touched and ignited fire.

Thunder shook its warning of the storm outside, but she paid it no heed, for a stronger storm was beginning to rage from within.

His heart played a staccato beat, and his breath against her face was labored and ragged. She felt her hair fall over his face as his lips opened wider, his kiss probing deeper. Her hands trailed down his face to his neck, where she slipped off his open tie and trailed her hand inside the collar of his shirt.

Suddenly his hands made contact. The touch frazzled her, set off alarms that warned of the danger in their reclined position. That voice cried out again, *beware!*

But she wanted to breathe more of the forest and herbs that teased her senses, wanted to taste more of the minty velvet of Sledge's mouth, wanted to feel more of the evening stubble chafing her skin. But frightening reality invaded her dream state when his hands came up once more to unclamp the strap of her dress.

She caught her breath. "This is going too far," she whispered, trying to push herself up.

He framed her face with his hands, and she felt him trapping her with his legs. "It can go so much further," he breathed. "I won't let you regret it, Kathy."

The muttering of the shortened version of her name caused a strange emotion to surface within her, and she closed her eyes against its power. But with the emotion came the defense barriers that she had trained to spring up when they were needed. She already did regret it. She regretted letting him mesmerize her in a way that could make her life miserable. She regretted the feelings coursing through her with the subtlety of a freight train. And most of all, she regretted that she would not make love to him tonight.

"I can't," she whispered.

"No, you can't," he agreed. "You can't pull away. You can't send me home. You can't deny what we feel for each other."

"I can't let this go on!" she insisted.

When she began to pull away, he covered his eyes with an arm, releasing her.

She sat up and tried to refasten her dress strap again. Giving up, she let it hang, hoping the secured catch on the other side was strong enough to keep her gown from falling.

Sledge sat up and combed both hands through his hair. He glanced over at her and closed his eyes as if her disheveled, flushed state was too much for him.

"I'm not a tease, Sledge, but I *am* human," she said with naked honesty.

A faint smile curved his lips. "Well, that's some consolation."

"I really mean it about getting tangled up with clients. It doesn't work, and I just can't do it."

Sledge shifted around to face her, and reached out to lift a curl of her hair. "But I don't have to be your client. You could tell Renfroe you're finished with me. Your rule wouldn't have to apply anymore."

Kathryn shoved his hand away with great effort. "No, Sledge. My work with you is a long way from being finished. I haven't even started working on your gestures or your expressions. I've just spent the past few sessions working on externals so that you could get the promos finished. Tomorrow we start on the important things."

Disbelief seeped into Sledge's face. "Who needs a cold shower? You can cool a guy off in five seconds flat. You're not really telling me there's more, are you?"

"A lot more. I've been studying the tapes of your interviews. Your manner puts people off. I want to work on that arrogance a little."

"Arrogance?" He clipped out the word, and she ignored the redness creeping up his neck, deciding that sort of heat was easier to handle than the one that had encompassed both of them only moments ago.

"Yes. And, as I've told you before, you put people on the defensive."

Sledge heaved a deep sigh and stood up, setting his hands on his hips. "People like you, for instance?"

"We're talking about the people you interview, Sledge."

"Are we really? I thought we were talking about why you're afraid to start something with me."

"I'm not afraid."

"Well, you sure do act like it. All I have to do is get too close and you act as if I'm trying to ruin your career. I have as much at stake in this hypothetical relationship as you do. Even more! It's not *your* personality that's being reshaped.''

"That's just it," Kathryn said, standing up to face him. "That's exactly why I won't get involved with you. Your personality is at stake. And your manhood is threatened. You have something to prove, Sledge. It happens to eighty percent of my clients, and it comes as no surprise.''

"Prove my manhood!" Sledge's voice gained volume. "Give me a little more credit than that, will you? I've never had to prove a damn thing to anyone. I think you're the one trying to prove something.''

"Like what?"

"Maybe you need to prove you've got this divine power that can change people. If you aren't in control, forget it. Maybe you won't get involved with anyone you haven't created yourself. Is that it?''

"No, that isn't it. But it's a little useless to start something with someone who has all the wrong motives.''

Sledge threw up his hands then slapped them down to his sides. "Lady, you sure don't have much faith in yourself if you think a man has to have ulterior motives for coming on to you. Are only lunatics allowed to see you as somebody special, somebody different? Do all the poor guys out there who've ever shown interest in you really have deep psychological problems?''

"That isn't what I said."

"But that's what you think," he said. "I'll tell you what. Tomorrow I'll sign up with a shrink, and I'll tell him that there must be something wrong with me because I'm attracted to a little spitfire named Kathryn Ellerbee."

And with that he slammed out of her apartment, leaving Kathryn staring at the door, with nothing left behind but his bow tie and her misery.

KATHRYN STOOD IN HER NIGHTGOWN at the sliding glass doors to her balcony, fingering the bow tie she held, and peered over the painted flowers on the glass to the rain slanting down to the ground. She opened the doors and stepped onto the wet balcony. Disregarding a puddle of rain, she sat down on one of the patio chairs.

The shelter overhead kept the rain from pelting her directly, but a thin mist dampened her skin. She pulled her feet up on the seat and looked at the black sky mottled with gray clouds. *Three in the morning,* she thought. *Everyone in the world must be asleep.* Everyone who didn't have demons and angels at war inside his head every time he closed his eyes.

Good Lord, she thought. Was Sledge right? Had she come to believe that only insecure clients could find her attractive? Had she convinced herself over the years that she wasn't worthy of real interest from a man?

It wouldn't be entirely her fault if that were true, she told herself. But years had passed since she'd really been hurt by one of those men attempting to prove something at her expense. And the scars had healed. But she was still afraid to trust.

Maybe tomorrow, she thought, looking up into the rain. Maybe tomorrow she'd give Sledge another chance. After all, she hadn't wanted to trust any other man as much. Maybe it was time she believed in herself for a change.

BUT BELIEVING IN HERSELF was a tough task when she had to face Sledge the next day.

"Are you ready for me?" Kathryn asked from his office doorway, when his silent, brooding acknowledgment of her presence led to no greeting at all.

Finally he reconsidered and set his work aside. "Why not?" he began. "What have I got to lose? Only a little arrogance, a little pride, a little—"

"Okay, Sledge," she said wearily, wheeling the television and VCR into the office with her. "I get the point. You don't plan to make my work easy today. I didn't expect you to."

Her unusually defeatist tone made him really look at her and survey the smudges of shadow under her eyes, proof that the events of the previous evening had not been conducive to a good night's sleep.

Ignoring his quiet scrutiny of her, Kathryn plugged in the television and closed the door. "I want to view some tapes with you this morning," she said. "They're of some of your problem interviews. I've been analyzing them."

"Studying me from a nice, safe distance, huh?" he added grimly.

Kathryn withstood his frosty gaze while she opened her briefcase and retrieved some video cassettes.

She turned back to him, and their eyes locked again. It was obvious they would get nothing done unless she could ease the tension between them. "Please." She made her appeal direct. "Can't we put last night behind us?"

"No problem," he said dourly. "Since you think it was all superficial, anyway, it should be easy to just forget."

She felt the weight of his grudging assessment. He was searching for a response that she could not provide.

"Real easy," Sledge continued harshly. "Just block from your mind the way we responded to each other, and hold on to the illusion that this potential mental patient bullied his way in last night and took advantage of you to feed his ego."

The static action on the television monitor added to the tension in the room. She felt the instinct to run, go home to bury herself under the covers in her bedroom and forget she'd ever met Darryl Sledge. But she was an adult, and adults didn't flee in the face of peril. They either faced it or replaced it with a more manageable risk.

Sledge's interview filled the TV screen, and absently Kathryn mumbled, "I want you to notice this cluster of forceful gestures. They denote a self-righteous attitude.''

From the corner of her eye she saw that his attention was focused on her, holding her in an almost tangible embrace. She felt *him* analyzing *her*, trying to break the code that held the key to her surrender. She struggled against letting him in. ''Sledge, please watch the tapes. I don't feel strong enough to fight you today.'' She felt the first ache of tears sting her eyes, tears that she could have fought off valiantly if she hadn't been so exhausted and emotionally raw. ''Staring at me is not helping my job—or my headache,'' she said, her weariness at the struggle apparent in her quiet voice.

Sledge issued a deep, rueful sigh, got up from behind his desk and went to her. Taking her shoulders gently, he turned her away from him. Slowly, sensuously, he began a massage, working out the fatigue that he had put there, inspiring fire to spark the places his fingers touched.

''Relax,'' he whispered as he kneaded the knots from her tense muscles. ''I didn't sleep last night, either.''

Kathryn dropped her head forward and focused on the floor, realizing that her silence was confirmation that thoughts of him had kept her awake last night. But she had no energy to deny it. Even if she'd had the physical strength, she was certain that in her emotional state, she couldn't reject his tenderness.

''The way you smell makes me dizzy,'' he whispered as his fingers worked their magic. He stepped closer, his chest barely brushing her back. "And that has nothing to do with either of our egos."

She closed her eyes and again felt shivers of fear and excitement scamper down her spine. The tape played on as he kneaded her shoulders and on down her arms, but she neither heard nor cared. She felt an irrational urge to sink back against him, to feel his strong arms fold her, to surrender and believe. . . .

A knock sounded on the door. Reluctantly Sledge ran his hand through Kathryn's hair and released her so that he could open the door.

Renfroe stood there, holding a popular local newspaper whose news had a reputation for being more gossip than fact. "Thought you'd both want to see this," he grumbled, thrusting the paper into Sledge's hands. "Not exactly what we had in mind when we assigned Kathryn to work with you." He wheeled around and started down the hall. "Page eight," he barked over his shoulder.

"Page eight," Sledge repeated, closing his door again and leaning against his desk as he thumbed through the pages. "Page—aw, damn!"

Kathryn looked over his shoulder and saw the printed photograph that had caught Sledge's attention. It was a picture of her standing between Sledge and Brad Miller, with Sledge's arm hooked over her shoulders and Brad handing her a drink. The caption read: "Two network favorites compete for same lady."

Kathryn reached for the paper. "I don't remember our pictures—"

Sledge's rage halted her words when he flung the paper across the room, only to have it land anticlimactically on the floor.

"What's the matter?" she asked, astounded. "Everybody knows it's just gossip."

"I don't want people thinking I have to fight a Milquetoast like Brad Miller for you! It's absurd! That's what's the matter!"

Tension crept back into Kathryn's muscles. "In the first place," she said pointedly, "I was his date. And in the second, I can't believe you'd suddenly start caring what people think about you! I've been trying to make you care about that ever since I started working with you."

Sledge swung around, the stiff set of his body warning that a fight was brewing. "I don't care what people think about my personality or the clothes I wear. But the very idea of me having to share you with Brad Miller!"

"You see?" Kathryn said, her cheeks beginning to flush with the dawning of understanding. "It *is* your ego. I was right. To think you'd almost convinced me that it was just me you liked, and not the challenge I represented. It's been your ego all along."

Some of the fury drained from his face, and his eyes widened in alarm. "Kathryn, it has not. That's not what I'm saying."

"It *is* what you're saying, Sledge. Whether you can see it or not, you just want to prove to the world that you can change the woman who tried to change you.

And then what would you do? Dump me and move on to the next challenge?''

"No. That's not—''

"I'm smarter than you think I am, Sledge. And I'm too smart to really believe that your attraction to me is real. *I'm* the one who needs to see a shrink. I almost let myself believe you!''

And with that she slammed out of the office, barreling down the corridor to the elevator before Sledge had the chance to come after her.

The trip home was a blur. When she reached the safety of her apartment Kathryn flicked on her radio, hoping to drown out the torrent of thoughts flooding her mind. She sank onto the sofa and hugged her knees to her chest. Their argument echoed through her head, causing a dull, aching emptiness from which she couldn't escape.

She recalled the feel of his hands kneading her shoulders, the husky sound of his voice when he'd told her that her fragrance made him dizzy. Then she relived their hopeless argument that seemed to have more to do with a relationship that would never be than it had with a picture in the paper.

She stretched out on the couch, aching with the need to cry and her inability to do so. She shouldn't be at home right now, she thought. She should be at the office, hurrying to finish the job so that she could put all thoughts of Darryl Sledge behind her. But she couldn't go back yet, she realized. Not until she was stronger.

For it seemed that, in spite of all her plans to revamp Darryl Sledge, it just wasn't working. She was the only one changing.

CHAPTER EIGHT

FROM THE SHALLOW DEPTHS of sleep, Kathryn heard a repetitive cereal jingle, a radio announcer's rapid-fire intro to an upbeat song and the foreign sound of a ringing bell. Stirring from the sofa, she reached for the telephone. A dial tone hummed out its nonchalance. Dropping the receiver back in its cradle, she cracked open her eyes and looked around to orient herself. She must have fallen asleep, she thought, glancing at the clock on her wall. The digital numbers read 2:00 P.M.

The doorbell rang again, startling her, and she pulled herself up, straightened her clothes and hair before stumbling to the door.

Brad Miller leaned against the doorjamb, wearing an open-necked denim shirt and faded jeans—the clothing of his television character—and an ever-so-proud-of-himself grin on his face. "Between you and your sister, I might not have any problems with my image, after all," he said confidently.

Kathryn motioned him in without enthusiasm. "So you and Amanda hit it off last night?"

"You know," he said, "she's a lot like you."

Kathryn couldn't believe her ears. "She's nothing like me, Brad. There is no one else like Amanda."

When Brad didn't make a move to sit down, and instead stood in front of her with a silly grin on his face, she groped for something else to say. "Anyway, I'm glad you had fun last night."

"I just hope you didn't mind my leaving you that way."

"It was my idea, remember?"

"Maybe. But I want you to know there's plenty of me to go around."

Kathryn had the sudden sickening feeling that the monster she had created was turning on her. "Wait a minute. You don't think—"

"I just don't want you to think I'm limiting my attention to one person." He closed the distance between them and narrowed his eyes in a way that she assumed was meant to be seductive.

"Amanda won't appreciate knowing that," she told him caustically.

"I won't tell her if you don't."

Wearily Kathryn held a hand out to stop him. "Brad, I'm not up to this. You're not interested in me."

"Oh, but I am. Now that the word's out in the newspapers that I'm officially wooing you—"

She slapped both hands against his chest and pushed—hard. "You are *not* wooing me. And a stupid picture in the tabloids doesn't—"

She halted her protest when he took her arms and pulled her against him, just as his television character would have done. Only this time she was the only director. "Brad Miller, get your hands off me immediately," she grated. "I don't want to hurt you."

"Don't fight it, Kat," he breathed.

"Don't call me Kat. My sister is the only one who calls me that. And you have two seconds to get your hands off of me!"

"A man can do a lot in two seconds," Brad said, and aimed a kiss that landed on her chin.

Suddenly the front door swung open, and Kathryn heard a loud gasp. "How could you?" Amanda cried. "I trusted you." At the sight of Amanda, Brad released Kathryn, and when she stepped back, she saw that Amanda's accusations were directed at her.

"How could *I*? Why don't you ask *him*, Amanda?"

Amanda glowered. "Working on his image, huh? Even the newspapers are onto you. If you'd wanted him, why didn't you just say so?"

Brad shrank against the couch, trying hard to look innocent, though he awaited Kathryn's answer with intense interest.

Kathryn slapped the heel of her hand to her forehead and wheeled on Brad. "Don't just stand there and let my sister think something's going on with us. Tell her the truth!"

"The truth," Amanda said, "is that he finagled me into his arms last night, and you today. I didn't expect him never to look at another woman again, but my own sister?"

Kathryn couldn't believe the day she was having. Briefly she eyed the phone book, wondering if bomb defusers were listed under *B* or *D*. "Amanda, you know me better than that. Since when have I gotten involved with clients?"

"How do I know?" Amanda sniped back. "Maybe it just took the right person!"

Brad's eyes widened, and he looked at Kathryn like a captivated spectator at a tennis match waiting for the return volley.

"If I were going to fall for a client, Amanda, it would not be him. It seems I've done too good a job on Brad. Without meaning to, I've turned him into a miserable, despicable, egotistical—"

"Did someone call me?"

The intruding voice drew all eyes to the open doorway. Sledge stood there in all his glory, taking in the scene, his amused grin absolutely incongruous in the context of the moment.

Kathryn threw up her hands and collapsed onto the couch. "Will one of you please tell me what I've done to deserve this day?" Sledge stepped inside, and Kathryn closed her eyes. "And what you just heard had nothing to do with you, Sledge."

"Oh. You mean there's more than one miserable, despicable—what was the other thing?"

"Egotistical," Brad provided sheepishly.

Sledge gave Brad a brief, assessing glance. "Yeah. You mean there's more than one like that?"

Kathryn groaned. "I was talking about Brad."

Sledge's humor faded, and he glared at the denim-clad man, who seemed to wear a little more self-confidence than he had the night before. "So now you're calling him names, too, huh?" An incredible note of jealousy rang in his voice, and it served to make Kathryn even more furious.

"I should be taping this," she mumbled. "No one would ever believe it."

"How come he gets to wear denim?" Sledge posed the question as if it were entirely relevant to the situation, and Kathryn sprang off the couch.

"I don't care what either of you wears! I've had it up to here with both of you!" she shouted, slashing a hand over her head. Kathryn grabbed Brad's arm and shoved him toward her sister. "If you want him, Amanda, here he is."

Amanda turned up her nose in disgust and went to the couch. "No. He's obviously made his choice."

"No, I haven't," Brad objected.

"What choice?" Sledge asked suspiciously.

Amanda jutted out her chin and managed to look hurt. "I suppose I had it coming to me. After all, I did horn in on her date last night."

Kathryn threw her hands over her face. "I can't stand this. She's done it to me since we were kids. Emotional blackmail."

Sledge, feeling that he'd missed something somewhere, turned to Amanda. "Will someone please tell me what's going on? It looks a little dangerous to draw my own conclusions around here."

Amanda shrugged dramatically. "Not much. I just walked in on Kathryn kissing Brad."

"That is not what happened!" Kathryn objected. "Brad was kissing *me*! He was trying to live up to his new image. Since the tabloids believe we're an item, he was trying to convince me! I told you, they call it transference. *I* call it an inflated ego."

An uncomfortable moment of silence followed, broken first by the nerve-racking chatter on the radio and then by Sledge. "There's a lot of that going around lately, huh?"

"An awful lot," Kathryn said. "And I'm getting a miserable headache. Don't you people have jobs? Can't you all go somewhere else to run me down?"

"Not until this is settled," Sledge said. He made straight for Brad. "So you came over here to practice those newfound techniques, huh, pal?"

Brad seemed to deflate visibly beside Sledge. "I just—"

"The lady was trying to do you a favor, and this is how you pay her back?"

"I didn't—"

"She helped you keep your job, and it probably wasn't all that easy. And what do you do?"

Brad swallowed and glanced toward Kathryn, then Amanda, with round, apologetic eyes.

"If I were you, buddy, I'd try to recoup my losses while I still had the chance. Women like Amanda don't wait around forever, you know."

Brad didn't answer.

"And guys like me don't have the market cornered on patience," Sledge continued in a calm but volatile voice. "I'd say it's time for you to make a clean exit."

Kathryn almost felt sorry for Brad as he approached Amanda, his face reddening. "I'm sorry, Amanda. I didn't mean to be such a jerk." And then he walked out, closing the door quietly behind him.

Amanda got up and dug in her purse for her car keys, then started for the door. "Thanks a lot, Kat," she said. "In just a few days you've turned Brad from a nice guy into an insensitive playboy. Just like my ex-husband. Did it ever occur to you that some people liked Brad the way he was?" Then, with a defeated slump to her shoulders, she left.

Kathryn began to massage her temples. "I believe it's your turn to make an exit," she said pointedly to Sledge.

"I'm staying," His eyes were as serious as she'd ever seen them, and for some insane reason, she wanted him to stay. But she had no room in her life for wishes that couldn't come true.

"No, you're not. I want you to go. I'm sick to death of fighting. Nothing's changed."

"I didn't come here to fight," Sledge said. "I came to apologize. I did let that article bruise my ego a little, but not in the way you think. And after seeing the scene that just took place here, I don't blame you for having trouble trusting my motives."

He touched her shoulder, but she turned away. Gently but firmly he turned her around to face him. "Kathy,

I've spent all day trying to figure out if you were right about me. You're not. I wasn't trying to prop up my ego. I was jealous of Brad, and it made me furious. It was a simple, human emotion.'' He stopped and inhaled deeply. ''The first night I saw you in the bar I was drawn to you. The place was a meat market where everyone looked and acted in the same predictable way. But you—you were different. You sat there as though you really didn't care whether anyone approached you or not, and I was intrigued. You had no intention of going home with me. And I had no intention of letting you out of my sight. I had absolutely nothing to prove then—but I was attracted to you. And you were attracted to me, too. Why can't we just back up and pretend we're just two ordinary people who met by chance?''

''Because we aren't,'' she whispered, shaken by the effect his words had on her. ''Because you're dangerous and I know better. And because there's more to a relationship than first impressions.''

''Sometimes first impressions are accurate. It's what comes later that screws everything up.'' He touched her hair, watched the lustrous play of light on it as he stroked it. ''Besides, I've had more than a first impression,'' he murmured. ''In fact, I have so many impressions of you whirling around in my head that frankly, they're driving me crazy.'' His hand swooped under her hair to cup her neck. ''And I don't know how much more I can stand.''

Kathryn read many things in his eyes—desire, frustration and intent. His face came closer, marked by vulnerability and uncertainty. He wanted her, yet he was giving her time to turn away.

She hesitated a moment too long before whispering, "Please don't kiss me."

"I have to," he answered, and his lips touched hers, more lightly than a sigh. They lingered only briefly, then retreated long enough for him to gauge her reaction. His thick spiky lashes fluttered against her cheek, and her lips parted in undisguised longing, offering the sign he'd been seeking.

His lips caressed hers, and they came tentatively together again. His hand moved to the back of her neck to draw her closer. With shaky fingers, she touched his face, memorized his features. He deepened the kiss, drawing her to him as he encompassed her, inspiring heat that could not be cooled, need that could not be sated. For a fragment of eternity the world ceased to exist, and they were alone in a dimension without logic or reason, where rules no longer seemed to apply. His arms were the fire that melted her fears, his breath the storm that stirred the elements within her, his kiss the rainbow that colored her heart with hope.

But that hope was as fleeting as the life of a rainbow, and it began to fade as his lips left hers. What was the difference? she asked herself, between his coming here and melting her heart, and Brad Miller's coming here to try? The only difference was that Sledge's methods were infinitely more effective. He'd warned her himself, the night they'd met, that awareness was no defense against his techniques.

Quietly she slipped out of his arms and broadened the distance between them.

"Even that didn't convince you?" he asked dolefully.

With difficulty, she dragged in a breath and shielded her transparent eyes with a trembling hand. "I take relationships very seriously, Sledge. They don't come easily for me."

"I take them seriously, too."

"No, you don't. You change women like socks. You haven't had a serious relationship in years."

Sledge grinned. "Would you believe that I've had one favorite pair of socks since I was sixteen? When I get attached, I really get attached." His smile faded, dissolving into deep, pensive lines around his eyes. He reached out for her hand and pulled her closer. "Tell me how long it's been since *you've* had a serious relationship."

Kathryn didn't answer.

"Years?"

She closed her eyes.

"Ever?"

"It's none of your business," she whispered.

"Yes, it is," he said. "If I'm going to be the first, it's absolutely my business." He let go of her hand and cupped her chin. "Look at me, Kathy."

Hesitantly she brought her weary eyes to his. "You aren't the first, Sledge. But I've learned from my past mistakes."

His eyes narrowed with understanding. "So he was a client, too, huh?"

She frowned up at him, wondering how Darryl Sledge had solved her puzzle. "Yes, he was," she admitted. "When I was just starting out. He was a politician, running for Congress. I worked very closely with him throughout his campaign, and I thought we had fallen in love with each other. I found out later that it wasn't love he had for me. He simply needed to prove a few things to himself. When he won the campaign, he was satisfied. He no longer felt he had anything to prove, and so our relationship was over."

Sledge gazed at her for a long moment. "That man was a fool, and I'll just have to convince you somehow that this time is different." He sculpted her cheek with the back of a finger, and she knew that if he kissed her again, she would be lost to him forever. But he didn't kiss her. Instead he breathed a long, choppy sigh and raised himself up as if he'd just come to a difficult decision. "I'm going now," he said. "You need time alone to think about what's happening here."

Her eyes grew doubtful as she struggled with the need to keep him with her, though denial scrambled for its own place in her heart. He dropped a kiss on her forehead, and went to open the door. "See you later, lovely lady," he whispered, and then he was gone, closing the door behind him.

Kathryn collapsed against the door and closed her eyes, squeezing back the tears and the frightening emotion that gripped her. How had he done this to her?

She went to the radio, turned it up louder and tried desperately not to think. But she had no more choice in what weighed on her mind, it seemed, than she had in the matters of her heart. Darryl Sledge had taken all her choices from her.

She went to the couch and curled up in the place where passion had lured them last night. The wish that the night had ended differently skittered through her mind before she could call it back. "Oh, Lord," she whispered, pinching the bridge of her nose. Had it already happened? Had he made her fall in love?

It was impossible, part of her argued. Didn't she know enough to avoid such a trap? Hadn't she trained herself better than that? She had spent years studying people and their behavior, anticipating their actions, interpreting their reactions. And she had enough insight into her own mind to realize that part of the reason for her studies had been to strengthen her own defenses against dangerous stimuli. Yet here she was, face-to-face with her own worst fear, and completely defenseless.

And was it really so bad? she wondered briefly. Wasn't it just possible that Sledge would take a relationship with her seriously?

Not on your life, came the answer in her mind. It was just a game with him. A psychologically motivated game that she had no choice but to fight. For he wasn't even aware of the fleetingness of his feelings for her.

Hours crept by, until the next morning dawned, more clearly defining the growing void in Kathryn's life. Unable to do otherwise, she went to work and resolved to keep her mind off her troubles, at least during the day. But it was impossible, because Sledge was a part of everything she did.

She sat alone in the network editing room that morning, viewing a taped interview that Sledge had done a few days earlier with the president of a company that was being sued for knowingly exposing its factory workers to asbestos poisoning.

"I have a list of seventy-five factory employees here," Sledge was saying, "who have been diagnosed as having asbestos-related diseases, and yet you're telling me that their sickness isn't related to their work environment?"

The company president squirmed in his chair. "I'm telling you that I don't know how they contracted those diseases."

Sledge leaned forward, facing the man squarely. "Then how do you explain the letter that passed between you and the board of directors ten years ago, saying that the company could not afford to correct the asbestos problems?"

The man hesitated and crossed his arms over his stomach. "I can explain it by saying that whoever gave you that letter is a liar. No such letter ever came from me."

"I didn't say it came from you, Mr. Winthrop. It was signed by your predecessor, but it was addressed to you, as well as several others in your company."

"If such a letter was written," Winthrop said, scratching his head, "I never saw it. I had no knowledge of it at all."

"Was there any discussion about how to handle the problem?"

"Not to my knowledge."

"Were you, the executive vice president, often left out of such important discussions?"

Good, Sledge! Kathryn thought. *Now lean back so he'll drop his guard a little.*

The man lifted his chin and said clearly, "I was never left out. My point is that none of us knew of the problem at that time."

As if he heard her order, Sledge leaned back in his chair and crossed an ankle over his knee. He began to tap his pencil eraser on his cheek. "I see," he replied in a voice that said, unequivocally, that he did not see at all. "Then I guess the obvious question is, why did management choose to put their offices in a building separate from the factory workers?"

The man scratched his nose and began to rub his cheek. "We were growing. We needed the room in the old building."

Don't let him get away with it, Kathryn thought.

"Let's be honest, Mr. Winthrop," Sledge said, giving a perceptive grin and uncrossing his legs. "Wasn't it really because you learned that your own president was dying of asbestosis and you didn't want to be exposed to the asbestos yourselves?''

"One thing had nothing to do with the other."

Sledge leaned forward and narrowed his eyes. "And even when you learned that your president had contracted the disease, you still didn't act to clean up the problem?"

"The company didn't have any more money to throw around just because our president was ill."

"In other words, you *did* know about it, and it did come down to a simple matter of money."

"No. That's not what I said."

Kathryn smiled. Sledge had cornered the man, cracked him, and she had not even had to tell him how to do it. Intuitively he had known the subtle signs to watch for. She flicked a button to back up the tape, and studied both men's body movements anew. Winthrop had brought his hand to his face with each answer, rubbing his nose or eyes, and he'd glanced away often, blinking more than usual. Sledge had reacted to those signals by facing him squarely, slowly increasing the pressure. And his obvious lack of belief had made the man fidget and sweat, so that anyone with intuitive sense could tell which man had something to hide. It wasn't until Sledge had got what he wanted from the man that he angled his body away, almost as if he were letting the man go, and the company president had sighed with obvious relief that the ordeal was over.

"And I didn't even have to tell him," Kathryn whispered to herself, feeling a swell of unaccountable pride.

He had known somehow. She rewound the tape back to the beginning, saw how the president had tried to establish a dominant position from the start, turning his palm downward as they shook hands. But just as she had advised in her book, Sledge had taken two steps toward him, forcing the hands to equal angles, subconsciously letting the man know that Darryl Sledge was, by no means, his inferior.

No one's inferior. And Kathryn was beginning to believe that he needed her professional advice like he needed a scholarship to charm school. The man had charisma and talent that needed no coaching. And his ego was secure enough that he had not let her attempts to redo him confuse him in the least about who or what he was.

"How's that asbestos story coming?" Renfroe interrupted her thoughts from the doorway. "Did he handle it all right?"

"He's a natural," she said, shutting off the tape machine. "I hate to say it, but I'm afraid you're wasting your money on me this time. It's taken some time for me to admit it, but Darryl Sledge is the last person I can think of who needs help with his image."

"Oh-oh." Renfroe plopped himself onto the chair next to her, and Kathryn could tell by his manner that something was wrong. "He's gotten to you, hasn't he?"

"What?" She looked at the producer, who was mangling a paper clip and peering at her unhappily.

"You're falling for him."

"I—what are you talking about?"

"I'm talking about this turnabout. One minute you're ready to beat him over the head with the changes I tell you to make and the next you think he's perfect. It doesn't take a genius—"

"I never said he was perfect," Kathryn cut in before he could finish. "I just think he has a certain charismatic style that is going to hook the viewers. He's been sure of that all along. Now I'm beginning to be convinced."

"Is that so?" Renfroe snapped the paper clip in two and shook his head dubiously. "Just the same, you're not finished with him until I say you are. And I'm not convinced yet."

Kathryn could tell that Renfroe had something up his sleeve. "So what do you want next?" she asked suspiciously.

"His name," Renfroe said. "We've been thinking about changing it—to Saxon."

"You're kidding!"

"Why? You don't like it?"

"I like his real name! So do a lot of other people who already know who he is."

"No problem," Renfroe said. "We'll simply tell everyone that Sledge was a television name and we've decided to go back to his original one."

"He'll never agree to it," Kathryn warned.

"He'll have to. He's not the one who calls the shots around here."

"And what will you do if he refuses? Fire him?"

"It won't come to that," Renfroe said smugly. "He knows which side his bread is buttered on."

Kathryn shook her head. "Obviously you don't. Mr. Renfroe, I want you to know that I'm absolutely against this. I think you should reconsider."

Renfroe stood up and treated her to a condescending smile. "I'll keep your opinion in mind, honey," he said as he sauntered out of the editing room.

Kathryn leaned forward and propped her elbows on the table. She rested her forehead against the heels of her hands and tried to put her feelings into perspective. She'd come to the conclusion that Sledge was fine the way he was, yet she had been hired to change him. She was a professional, and she was good at her job.

Or she had been once. Squeezing her eyes shut, she tried to remember her objectives when she'd come off the lecture circuit after her book was first published. She'd wanted to help people who needed help. She'd planned to teach them how to say, through word and gestures, what they really meant, without sending a lot of extra signals that confused the subconscious of the people they were speaking to. She had never intended to break into the personalities of her clients and try to re-program them. She had never meant to teach people not to be themselves.

But that was all she'd done lately. She'd tried to change the very thing in Sledge that made him unique among all the other television broadcasters she'd seen, and she'd forced an image on Brad Miller that he simply did not know how to deal with.

Why? she asked herself. Was it simply because the network had told her to? She'd had more integrity than that when she'd started out. Surely she'd worked too hard to be little more than a network puppet!

She heard footsteps behind her, and suddenly a pair of strong, rugged hands began to massage her shoulders. "Why the sad eyes?" Sledge asked against her ear. "My interview wasn't that bad, was it?"

"No," she said, trying to make her voice sound bright. "It was good. You did everything I would have told you to do."

"You did tell me," he said. "I told you I read your book. It had some good pointers."

She nodded and flicked the tape back on to call his attention away from her. "You've really got a passion for your work, don't you, Sledge?"

"I have a passion for a lot of things," he said.

When she didn't answer, Sledge stepped around her and turned the machine off, then leaned against the table facing her. "So what's the matter? Is it your sister?"

Although her sister was not the real reason for the turmoil she was feeling, Kathryn nodded. "Well, she's still not speaking to me. It's all right, though. She hates me for at least three weeks a year altogether."

"I saw Miller in the lobby this morning," Sledge said, satisfied that he was on the right track. "It seems the man wants to call her, but feels he blew it. Poor guy actually looked humble."

"He's really a sweet guy who has no business pretending to be a sex symbol," Kathryn said. "He can't fit into that mold, and it can only end in disaster. The only reason he got the leading role in his soap in the first place was that the real hero went off the show."

Sledge studied the worry lines on her face. After a moment he pushed off from the table and sat down in the chair Renfroe had recently abandoned. "You know, I've been thinking. If Brad had one woman, maybe people wouldn't expect him to act like a stud."

Kathryn clenched her fist. "Exactly. And if I were a decent image consultant, I would have found some way to make his new image fit him, instead of making him fit some contrived image. I must have been crazy."

"You were just doing your job," Sledge said in her defense. He thought for a moment longer, before a hopeful light perked up his eyes. "I'll tell you what. You come to Steppin' Out tonight at seven o'clock. I'll solve all your problems. I promise."

"At Steppin' Out?" She was genuinely confused. "What are you going to do? Get me drunk so I can forget them?"

"My intentions are honorable," Sledge said mysteriously. "Just be there at seven. And trust me."

CHAPTER NINE

JUST AS IT HAD BEEN the night she'd met Darryl Sledge, Steppin' Out was a polyglot of lustrous smiles, eloquent eyes and laughing conversations between friends old and new. Tina Turner's voice reigned in an upbeat, blood-pumping rhythm, and couples responded by filling the dance floor and moving with provocative flair beneath a strobe light.

The blond bouncer imposing order on the place gave Kathryn a bold wink, which she politely ignored. The crimson dress she wore highlighted the color in her cheeks and drew second looks from the men at the bar, but she had worn it tonight to impress one man only. With eyes bright and glittering with purpose, she sought out that man.

As she expected, he sat at his place at the bar, but instead of a newspaper, Darryl Sledge had a buxom blonde as his focus. A surge of jealousy shuddered through Kathryn's veins as she watched Sledge's shoulders move with subtle laughter. The woman puffed up her bosom and tried to look indignant. He smiled that your-place-or-mine smile, and Kathryn could almost hear him using the lines on the blonde that he had used on her: "Details. It's not your name I want to take home."

Was this his idea of taking care of everything! Was this why he'd asked her to trust him? A sudden, irrational urge to march over to the woman and scratch out her baby blues filled her, but Kathryn's more pragmatic side quelled the impulse as unacceptable behavior. Running home was another possible solution, she told herself. But her pride squelched that idea. The least she could do was make Darryl Sledge feel like a rat, if rats, indeed, had consciences.

Almost as if her thoughts had touched him, Sledge swiveled away from the woman at his side and looked toward the door. Their eyes met, his warm and smiling, Kathryn's cold and piercing, and she walked to a vacant table without giving him the benefit of acknowledgment.

Without saying goodbye to the woman, who watched with a regretful shake of her head, he left the bar and sauntered toward Kathryn, drink in hand. "You could start a brawl in that dress," he drawled as he pulled out a chair.

"And you could start a scandal with the company you keep," she shot back.

"Who, you?" The question was genuine.

"No. Miss Peroxide over there."

Sledge glanced over his shoulder to the woman in question and brought searching eyes back to Kathryn. "Oh, her. Jealous, are we?"

"No, we are not! *We* are just wondering why *we* were asked to come here."

"Well, certainly not so that I could pick up women in front of you."

"I see," Kathryn said, nodding. "Then it was a spur of the moment decision."

"I was not picking her up." The amusement sparkling in his eyes counteracted the firmness of his voice. "She asked me a question. I answered her."

"Did she ask you to guess how many freckles she has on her chest?" Kathryn said sarcastically. "That would explain why your eyes were where they were."

Sledge tipped his chair back and gave in to a full, tumbling laugh. "Little lady, you're so jealous those beautiful black eyes of yours are turning green. The woman did not interest me at all, and I was not looking at her chest, despite how much she wanted me to. She fed me the most unoriginal line in the book. She asked me what my sign was. I told her No Smoking, and she laughed. That was all."

"Oh? And did she tell you her sign?"

Sledge gestured toward the woman, who was dressed in hot pink. "Neon, obviously."

Kathryn fought back the smile straining to break through her countenance. The transparency of her jealousy made her feel a little foolish.

"Not like yours," he said, cupping her chin and rubbing his thumb along her bottom lip. "Yours says, Danger—Proceed at Your Own Risk."

"Risk of what?" she asked.

"Risk of losing yourself, your mind, your heart..."
His voice trailed off and he feathered a kiss across her
lips, and she knew, without thinking, the risks he spoke
of. "Your arrogance, your ego, your heart," he tacked
on. "Your accent, your mustache, your heart."

She tried to speak, to object, but her heart seemed to
be caught in her throat.

"It's okay," Sledge said. "I'm going to redeem myself tonight. I invited Brad and Amanda here. I'm going
to get them back together so all your worries will be out
of the way and you can concentrate on falling in love
with me."

"Sledge—" She felt her cheeks stinging and her heart
pounding.

"It's only fair," Sledge insisted. "One heart for another."

She was trapped again—trapped in the Sledge-world
that warmed and surrounded her. Trapped in the intent
of eyes as blue as an ocean sky, trapped in the promise
of full lips descending to hers, trapped in the hope of a
touch that bestowed only truth.

But the world popped like an overinflated balloon
when a long hot-pink fingernail tapped on Sledge's
shoulder, destroying the tension and magic swelling between them.

"My phone number." The blonde from the bar
stuffed a small piece of paper into Sledge's shirt pocket,
then patted his hard, broad chest. "In case you have

regrets,'' she said before slinking off like a cat, leaving Sledge and Kathryn gaping after her.

"Uh, where were we?" As if to reorient himself, Sledge took hold of Kathryn's hand.

"Where were we?" She jerked her hand out of his. "We were exchanging hearts, I believe."

"What just happened was not my fault."

"Give me a break, Sledge. Somewhere that woman got the idea that you were interested in having her phone number. I'm a big believer in reading between the lines, but even I don't think that a woman can glean 'What's your phone number?' from 'No Smoking.'"

Sledge's eyes frosted over, and he slammed his hands on the table.

"Tell me you're not calling me a liar."

"I am, Sledge," she admitted defiantly. "Only unlike Freda Lynn Anderson, I can pronounce my *l*'s!"

"I warned you . . ." he began, jerking her closer to him.

"Try it, buster!" she bit out. "You might have to give up those lips after all!"

Sledge recognized the fire in her eyes, and let her go. "You really think I'd come on to some woman, knowing you were coming here? After all I've done to make you trust me?"

"I'm just saying that you left something out. Like the part where you propositioned her—perhaps as a backup in case I didn't come around? To prop up your flagging ego in case I injured it too badly?"

Sledge's eyes dulled over, and he scooted back from the table. "Lady, as hard as you've tried to injure my ego, I assure you it isn't done for yet. And if you've finished lashing out at me because some stupid blonde ruffled your feathers, I'm going to rescue Brad Miller from himself and try to make some sense of the mess things have been since the night we met!"

It was all Kathryn could do to keep from shouting something foolish, childish and satisfying at his back. She saw him pushing through the crowd toward Brad, who stood in the doorway, searching the dark room from behind even darker glasses that drew more attention than they diverted.

Cool handshakes were exchanged, and then Brad and Sledge started back toward Kathryn. She considered leaving, but decided it would make things too easy for the man who was turning her world upside down.

"I thought you said Amanda was coming," Brad said when he'd sat down. He took off his glasses and revealed his squinting, contact-ridden, pseudo-blue eyes.

"I told her to come a little later so I'd have the chance to talk to you first," Sledge said dully, as if he'd been robbed of his enthusiasm. "I had to make sure you wanted another chance with her."

"Want one? Are you kidding?"

"I take it that means yes?" he asked with an obvious lack of patience.

"Of course. I'm crazy about her. But she'll probably never speak to me again. I've been such a jerk."

Kathryn turned her head away. She wasn't going to touch that line.

"Well, pal, that's up to you," Sledge advised. "You've got to convince her that you're not after anything in skirts, including her sister and my lady."

Kathryn's eyes shot to his, suddenly flashing out a defensive burst of fire. "I'm not your—"

"And I'm going to convince you," Sledge told Brad, forging ahead without heeding Kathryn's protest. "But first, why don't you pop out those lenses? Surely blindness is preferable to squinting all the time. Believe me, I've had blue eyes for thirty-four years, and I've never felt their benefits were worth that much trouble."

Brad grimaced. "But the network wants—"

"Sometimes you've just got to ignore the network."

Kathryn compressed her lips and bristled. He was undermining her authority, and the most infuriating part of it was that he was right.

"But my eyes are gray," Brad went on. "They look like rocks."

Sledge gave Kathryn a false smile. "Congratulations. You've done some kind of job on this guy." He turned back to Brad. "Man, it's better to have eyes that look like rocks than to have eyes that feel like they have rocks in them. If being blue eyed makes you miserable, who the hell cares what the network thinks?"

Brad looked to Kathryn for permission.

"Brad," Sledge continued, "if you want to be more attractive to the ladies, keep the gray eyes. Women like earthy looks. I can't think of anything more earthy than rocks."

Again Brad sought Kathryn's approval. "Take them out if you want to," she told him finally. "You don't have to ask my permission."

Relief emanated from Brad like a tangible thing, and pulling a lens carrying case from his shirt pocket, he popped out his contacts.

Amazingly Brad's eyes did look better gray than they did blue.

"Now that that's out of the way," Sledge said, "I want to talk to you about the image you've been trying to live up to."

Kathryn waved to the barmaid. She could tell she was going to need a drink for this one.

As Sledge settled back in his chair like an old world-weary adviser, the barmaid came to the table. "White wine, please," Kathryn told her.

Sledge got right down to business. "First of all, Miller, I'm here to tell you that playboydom isn't all it's cracked up to be. I know what it's like to have women calling in the middle of the night."

"Make that a double," Kathryn called to the barmaid.

Sledge lost his train of thought as her words filtered through to him. "A double white wine?"

"Whatever it takes," she said. "Go on. You were complaining about the hordes of women who call you in the middle of the night."

Sledge ignored her sarcasm and turned back to Brad. "Yes. And believe me, it's no fun. All it gets you is misunderstood."

"Misunderstood?" Kathryn echoed incredulously.

Sledge stomped down on her foot under the table, warning her that the floor was his. Fortunately for everyone involved, the barmaid chose that moment to bring Kathryn's wine.

"It gets out of hand after a while," Sledge continued, "and before you know it, all kinds of women are asking you to count their freckles, stuffing phone numbers in your pockets and pestering you with intimate talk about astrological signs."

Kathryn took a gulp of wine to keep herself from butting in. Brad struggled to follow Sledge, but the blank look on his face spoke of his confusion.

"Anyway," Sledge went on, "the point is that there comes a time when you don't even see the ladies smiling your way anymore, because you've seen so many of them. They begin to look the same to you, and you start to think back over all the wasted years and wonder what it would have been like if there had been just one woman." His voice lost its commercial quality and took on a sincerity that Kathryn wondered if she was imagining. "Because with one woman you can build something. You can invest your time in each other, and then when the day comes to look back, there'll be good things to remember. Not a series of wasted nights."

He sounded almost serious. He looked serious, and Kathryn couldn't help studying him for some sign of facetiousness. But there was none.

"Are you telling me to marry Amanda?" Brad asked from out of the blue.

Sledge inclined his head and rubbed the spot above his lip, frowning. "I hate to break it to you, Brad, but the two of you would have to at least be on speaking terms to get married. I'd say you should just improvise, quit waiting for some director to jump out and say, 'Action!'"

"Surely you're not telling me just to live with her!"

Sledge wilted and looked hopelessly at Kathryn. "The best laid plans of mice and men," he said, giving up.

Kathryn tried not to smile. She had to hand it to Sledge. He had tried, and it hadn't been easy. Just then a flash of gold appeared at the doorway, and Amanda stood in front of the bouncer. "You might need to put those sunglasses back on, Brad," Kathryn warned. "Amanda's here, and she's a little bright tonight."

Brad's expression lightened appreciably as he sighted the bold beauty in her gold lamé sweatshirt that exposed one flirty shoulder, and her tight black pants. One side of her hair was pulled back from her face, but the rest shimmered to her shoulders, Cleopatra-style. "If being with her doesn't improve my image," he said in an awestruck voice, "I don't know what will. But how do I know she won't take one look at me and run, after what I did?"

"Oh, she's explosive," Kathryn said. "But her temper tends to burn itself out. All it takes is an apology—or two. Or three."

"Come on." Sledge stood up and patted Brad's shoulder. "I'll be the buffer, since this whole thing was my idea. I've been dodging verbal punches from Amanda's sister for a while now. Maybe I can block some of the worst ones for you."

Kathryn ignored the comment and sipped her drink. An old Beatles song about a weeping guitar wafted through the room with appropriately depressing chords as the two men pushed toward her sister. It was obvious from the way Amanda snubbed Brad that she didn't want him to think she had come to see him, and pulling out a cigarette, she led the men toward the bar and ordered herself a drink.

Kathryn didn't know why she found Amanda's nonchalance so amusing, but she covered her smile with the tips of her fingers. Sledge stood between the two of them, rubbing his forehead as if he'd had as much as he could take from all of them, but still he continued talking to her sister, pleading with her, Kathryn was sure, and meeting with a dead end. If Kathryn knew her sister, and she did, Amanda would not speak to Brad until she was satisfied that she'd made him suffer.

Suddenly Amanda's shoulders lifted exaggeratedly. She mumbled something haughtily to Sledge and started toward Kathryn. As she plopped herself down in the chair across from her sister, her glittery, striped eyelids lowered with irritation. "What's his problem?" she asked, as if the days of not speaking had never occurred. "He told me that if I didn't come over here and apologize to you he would tell Brad I watched MTV instead of daytime drama."

"So are you?" Kathryn asked.

"Am I what?"

"Apologizing?"

Hedging, Amanda searched her clutch purse for another cigarette, then gave her sister an assessing look. "He's a catch, you know. I know a catch when I see one."

"Who, Brad?" Kathryn asked, but she knew perfectly well whom they were talking about.

"I'm talking about Sledge. And he likes you—a lot."

"Yeah? Me and everybody else who bats her eyes at him. He thinks if he conquers me it'll tell the world that he's flawless."

"Kat, you're rationalizing. I hate it when you rationalize."

"I'm facing the facts."

Amanda lit her cigarette and took a long drag, which came out in a crooked ring. "You want facts, my dear little sister? His exact words when he called me today were 'I've got it bad for your sister, and I want you and Miller off her mind so she can just worry about fighting me.'"

"Exact words?" Kathryn asked without conviction. "I'll buy the part about his wanting you off my mind. He thinks I've been crushed that you weren't speaking to me. He doesn't realize that fury and occasional silences are vital aspects of our relationship." Amanda caught her sister's smile and pursed her lips to keep from laughing. "But the part about his having it bad? Forget it. Sledge would never say that."

"He said it. Like it or not." Amanda set her cigarette on the ashtray without putting it out. "You just don't want to believe it. You think that if you do, you'll have to take a chance. And taking chances means risking failure. You don't like failure."

And who did? Kathryn thought as she grabbed Amanda's burning cigarette and butted it out roughly. "I hate it when you let these things burn. Haven't you ever heard of putting them out? You think I like sitting here watching them shrivel up?" She'd overreacted— and she knew it. Worse, so did Amanda. Her laughing eyes made that crystal clear. "I'm not afraid of taking chances, Amanda. I'm just having trouble believing the odds are on my side. I've been through this before, remember?"

Amanda nodded. "I remember. But you were younger and more vulnerable then. You know a lot more now."

"Enough not to make that mistake again."

Amanda shook her head regretfully. "I never had you figured for a coward, Kat."

Kathryn took refuge in her wine, but when her sister didn't loosen her visual grip, she set the glass down. "Then you had me figured wrong."

Amanda gave a grand shrug. "It's your life," she said, as if it didn't affect her at all. "But I'm telling you—Sledge is different. I've been around the block a few times, Kat. I've met a lot of different types, and Sledge is genuine. He's exactly what he appears to be. It's time you started to see that.''

"Sometimes I do," she said on a sigh, glancing over at the man who had her life mixed up like a defective micro chip. "And then something happens, and everything changes."

"That's because you're looking for something to happen, to get you off the hook. Take me and Brad, for instance. I could take what he did as some omen, if I were as afraid of getting involved as you are, but I don't have time to worry about things like that. I prefer to put it behind us and move ahead." Her face became truly animated. "I really, really like him. That night after the party we sat in his car in front of my house, and we talked for hours. He was interesting, and he thought I was, too. Now how many playboys would want to sit in a car and just talk?" She took a sip of her drink and pondered the situation. "I may have been off base when I accused you of changing him," she began carefully. "But I've had a playboy, Kat. Deep down, maybe I'm still some kind of homebody who wants just one man I can depend on. It hurt to think Brad might not be that man. But it's easy to get caught up in what's expected of you, so I'm willing to let his little mistake go by this time." She considered the brooding actor, who sat slumped at the bar. "What do you think? Have I let him sweat long enough?''

Kathryn smiled. "Amanda, show a little mercy. Don't make the man grovel."

"I was about to give you the same advice," Amanda said. "But I don't play games. I just wanted to give him time to think about what he was losing if he chose to play the field. Catches like me don't come around every day, you know. It's time he realized that."

Kathryn nodded agreement, but her mind was on the other man at the bar, the one who leaned against it, his fingers making horizontal strokes beneath his nose, his serious, pensive blue gaze locking with hers.

"Oh, well," Amanda said, clinking glasses with her sister. "Here's to us. May we each get what we want, whether we know we want it or not. And now it's time to reel in my line." With that, she was out of her chair, stalking toward the dejected-looking soap star, who was absolutely oblivious to what he was in for.

Sledge was already on his way to Kathryn's table. "So," he said, swirling his drink around in his glass. "For the sake of inspiration for our stumbling couple, how about dancing with me? Maybe Miller'll take the hint and ask your sister."

Kathryn was quite sure that if he didn't, Amanda would not hesitate to get him on the dance floor herself. "I've never danced with you before" was the most intelligent thing she could manage to say when she saw the vulnerability in Sledge's eyes.

"I'm no Fred Astaire, but I haven't had that many complaints," Sledge said, holding out his hand to her.

She took it and stood up. "All right."

He led her to the dance floor, then drew her near him as a song about a long-ago love began to play. It filtered into Kathryn's thoughts, with the message somehow applying to her present state of mind, for she felt as if she'd known Sledge a lifetime. His hands were crossed behind her waist, and she moved her own to his shoulders, lingering on hard, well-defined biceps along the way before clasping her hands behind his neck.

Their eyes collided for a jolting moment, his soft-blue regretful gaze wreaking havoc in her heart. She longed for him to say something, some cute line that would break the tension, give her an opening to apologize for misinterpreting his conversation with the blonde, but he didn't say a word. His eyes were bare, honest, full of vulnerability, which told her his happiness was in her hands.

She didn't know if her feet were moving, for she was so lost in the magic of Sledge's warmth that the music only seemed an extension of him. She pressed her face against his shoulder, felt the beat of his racing pulse hammering out the words, *trust me, trust me.* And she knew that this would be the night of her surrender.

Another couple bumped them, startling her out of her fantasy, and Kathryn turned to see Amanda winking at her over Brad's shoulder. Brad was holding Amanda possessively, and Kathryn had to admit that he was the perfect picture of Hollywood pizzazz with her sister in his arms.

The song ended, and Sledge noticed Brad and Amanda together. "The deed's done. They're dancing. Guess they're on their own now."

Kathryn's heart two-stepped in anticipation of what was to come, but Sledge simply led her back to her table and picked up his drink. "I haven't paid my tab yet," he said, and with eyes more serious and fragile than she had ever seen them before, he went back to the bar.

She watched him pay his bill, but her heart sank when he sat down on his barstool and stared into his drink as if it were the only place he could look for answers. She had been wrong to question his motives, she told herself. He had really not done anything wrong. On the contrary, he had tried to make things right for her—so she could concentrate on falling in love with him. He should have known that falling in love with him took no concentration at all.

Amanda tapped her on the shoulder and gave her a quick wave as Brad tugged at her hand. "We're out of here," she whispered. "And tell that big hunk at the bar that I owe him one. If he demands my sister as payment, I will have no choice but to sign you over." And with a farewell wink, Amanda locked arms with Brad and disappeared into the crowd.

Kathryn looked back at Sledge and saw him bottom his drink and turn to face her with an evaluating look. For a moment she feared he would leave, and relief washed over her as he set down his glass and sauntered toward her.

Nervously she played with her wineglass, struggling to find the right words, but her heart ran a wild race that left her speechless. She smiled shyly up at him. His eyes remained serious, penetrating into her with bold depth. Slowly, hypnotically, he leaned across the table, bracing himself with bent arms, until his face was no more than inches away from hers. "Next move is yours, sweetheart," he whispered.

And before she could catch her breath, he was heading for the door.

CHAPTER TEN

KATHRYN SLAMMED HER APARTMENT DOOR in frustration, and wondered how in the world Sledge expected her to make the next move when she didn't even know where the man lived! His phone number hadn't been listed yet, and the business office at the station was closed for the day. She didn't have a clue where to look for him. If his stalemate hadn't come as such a surprise, she would have followed him. But by the time she'd been physically able to react, he'd gone.

If he had just given her the chance, she railed mentally. If he had just let her tell him that she was sorry for her accusations. *But he did give you the chance,* she told herself. *Over and over and over.* Furiously she bolted into her bedroom and jerked the cardboard Sledge out of her closet, then stood back looking at it, as if it were Sledge himself.

"So you've finally got me where you wanted me, haven't you?" she accused. "Head over heels in love, without a rational thought in my head, without one iota of self-confidence to back me up. You've even got me standing here babbling at a stupid poster, wondering where in the world you are!" She coiled her hands into fists and let out a frustrated scream. "You're driving me crazy, Darryl Sledge! I might as well admit I'm in love with you to save my sanity. I might as well just dive in headfirst and admit it." She set her hands on her hips and lifted her chin defiantly. "Okay, so I'm in love with you. Unconditionally, absolutely, heart-wrenchingly in love. So what are you going to do about it?"

The cardboard likeness only grinned, prompting her to collapse onto the bed, her spirit deflated. "No, Kathryn Ellerbee," she said, mocking Sledge's voice, "the question is, what are *you* going to do about it?"

"I don't know!" she shouted. "I've never been in this situation before. I'm always on the running end. I don't even know how to chase!" She sat up on the edge of her bed and took deep, cleansing breaths to control herself.

"Just calm down," she ordered herself. "Think rationally. Morning will come soon. And then you can march into his office and tell him how you feel." She looked at her watch and moaned. "It's only eight short hours away."

Silently she resolved to stop talking to herself before her neighbors called in the men with the straitjackets. Instead she'd talk to Amanda. The woman owed her one, after all.

She went to the phone and punched out Amanda's number, then cringed as her sister's breathy recorded voice said, "I'm not home right now, but I'd love to know you called. Leave your name, phone number, height, weight, hair color and net worth at the sound of the beep, and I'll get back to you as soon as I verify it.''

Kathryn rolled her eyes. She'd forgotten that Amanda rarely answered the phone, especially when she had company. The tone sounded, and she sputtered, "Amanda, it's me. What tastes better? Cyanide or Liquid Plumber? Don't worry, it's not urgent. I'm under control.''

There, that ought to do it, Kathryn thought as she returned the phone to its cradle. If Amanda and Brad were there, then her sister would arrive here in say, ten minutes. A surge of guilt shot through her, but she vetoed it. She was desperate, and she needed Amanda. How else was she going to figure out how to make that next move? And what on earth were sisters for, if not to share moments of panic?

Twelve minutes later, a loud knock sounded on the door. Amanda looked relieved when Kathryn let her in. "Okay," she said, still panting. "I guess I deserved it for all the little bombs I've dropped on you through your answering machine. But for heaven's sake, Kat! Cyanide? For all I knew you were serious!''

"I was serious," Kathryn said, closing the door as her sister scuffed in and sank onto the couch.

"Okay," Amanda said, her breath returning to normal. "Let's hear it. What happened?''

"Nothing happened—that's just it! When you and Brad left, Sledge came over looking as if he would sweep me off my feet, and he informed me that the next move was mine.''

"And?"

"And he left!"

"That's it?" Amanda asked with disbelief. "You made me leave Brad Miller for that?"

Kathryn started toward her bedroom. "Thanks a lot, Sis. You're a real help."

Amanda pulled herself up from the couch and followed her. "Well, didn't you go after him? Didn't you make that move?"

"No," Kathryn said, seriously considering the cyanide, after all. She went to her dresser and pulled out the bow tie she had removed from Sledge's neck the night of the party, and the leopard-skin briefs he had given her. "I was dumbfounded. Now I have to think of something drastic to get him back, but I'm fresh out of ideas. He's driving me crazy. Absolutely crazy." Going back to the poster, she gazed up into the eyes that melted her heart even in a photograph and wrapped the bow tie around his neck. Then, stuffing the briefs in his hand, she stood back to examine her handiwork.

"Keepsakes?" Amanda asked frivolously. "What did you do? Demand a different piece of clothing every time he came over?"

Kathryn shot her an unappreciative look. "No. He gave these to me."

"Just volunteered them, did he?"

Kathryn cast up a silent prayer for patience. "Are you going to help me or not, Amanda?"

"Well, if anyone knows about chasing down men, I do," Amanda admitted. "And if we hurry, I can make it back before Brad gives up on me. I'm not sure, but I think he was on the brink of proposing. He was getting serious, you know? He was telling me something about wanting to build a relationship instead of a series of wasted nights. And you thought he was shallow.''

Kathryn decided not to tell her sister that those loving words had come from Sledge's lips. She suspected it didn't matter, anyway.

Pulling out a cigarette and lighting it, as if it could help her to think, Amanda surveyed the handsome pose of the man in question. ''You look like you need a mate,'' she told the poster. ''We'll have to see what we can do about that.''

Rushing to Kathryn's dresser, she pulled one drawer open and rummaged through the clothes until she came up with a pair of cutoff jeans. She tossed them over her shoulder to Kathryn and kept on digging. ''Put those on,'' she ordered.

''Why?''

''Just do it.''

Kathryn felt she had nothing to lose, so she slipped off her dress and pulled on the shorts. Amanda handed her a white tank top that hadn't been worn since it had shrunk in the dryer. ''Perfect,'' she exclaimed. ''Put it on.''

''But I don't wear that anymore. It's too tight.''

''It's just what we want,'' Amanda assured her, shoving her sister out of the way as she made a beeline for the closet.

Feeling a bit apprehensive, Kathryn slipped on the shirt. "It's indecent," she said, looking down at the way it clung tightly to her breasts. "If you're planning to take me out in this, you're going to be disappointed."

"We won't leave the apartment," Amanda assured her, and pulled out a pair of designer cowboy boots. "So here's where I left these! Why didn't you tell me they were here?"

"Because I had hoped you'd quit wearing them," Kathryn said frankly. "And if you think I'm going to—"

"Come on, Kat. Do you want to look like a woman of the eighties or a woman *in* her eighties?"

"It depends. Who's going to see me?"

"It depends," Amanda mocked. "How bad do you want Sledge?"

With a frustrated groan, Kathryn snatched the boots from her sister and shoved her feet into them. "What else? I have a pair of fake glasses with a big nose attached around here somewhere."

"This!" Amanda crowed with delight. She pulled out a cowboy hat that one of Kathryn's clients had given her. Setting it on Kathryn's head at a jaunty angle, she stood back and clapped her hands together. "It's absolutely perfect!" she said. "Now where's your camera?"

"My what?"

"Your camera. You can only fight drastic measures with drastic measures. We're going to send Darryl

Sledge a poster of you. And if he doesn't read the message loud and clear, the man's not worth it.''

Understanding dawned in Kathryn's eyes, and she got her camera and gave it to Amanda. "You're a genius," she told her sister, as she struck a pose that would put Darryl Sledge to shame and grinned the way he had the first night in the bar when he'd said, "Thought you might want a closer look." She'd never known then that taking a closer look would cost her her heart and everything that went along with it. But the price had been paid, and she hoped to exact a price in return. *One heart for another.*

The lightning flash of the camera brightened the room for a second, capturing Kathryn's likeness. "Sledge doesn't know what he's getting into," Amanda said as she snapped a few more pictures—just in case. "He hasn't got a chance."

KATHRYN HAD HER FILM at the photographers' the moment they opened the next morning, and she paid them an exorbitant amount to get a stand-up poster of her made by that afternoon. Then she rushed to the network building and toward Sledge's office, to make the move that she had thought about all night, but Renfroe's secretary stopped her and told her the producer wanted to see her—immediately.

"We've made the final decision," he said, opening a pack of antacid tablets. "We're changing Sledge's name to Saxon today."

Kathryn shook her head in amazement. "I've told you over and over, I'm completely against this. It won't work."

"Of course it will. Would you take a guy seriously who was named Sledge?"

"I already have," she pointed out. "And so have you, or you wouldn't have hired him. Sledge can carry this show without gimmicks. He's good at what he does. I'm beginning to wonder if he couldn't have made *InSight* a hit the way he was, without any changes at all. He's different, and that makes him stand out."

"I was right," he said with disgust. "You're falling for him, aren't you?" The observation dropped like lead between them.

Kathryn reminded herself not to get into a no-win situation with the likes of Renfroe. "I'm talking in professional terms, Mr. Renfroe. I've been hired to give advice, and I'm giving it."

"You've been hired to give the advice we tell you to give."

Kathryn reminded herself that her whole contract with the network was at stake. "I'm not the network puppet," she said slowly. "I'm an expert in my field, and as an expert, I refuse to have anything to do with changing Sledge's name."

"It'll be changed with or without you," Renfroe promised, rubbing his reddening face with a callused hand.

"Fine," Kathryn said, standing up. "Then it will have to be done without me."

"I'll do it myself," Renfroe threatened, eyes glaring.

"You've run out of puppets already? Well, good luck. You're going to need it."

She started out of the producer's office, intent on making it to Sledge in time to warn him before things blew up, but Renfroe bolted past her. "Where's Sledge?" he boomed to his secretary.

"In the studio," the woman said.

Renfroe flashed Kathryn a look and barreled around the corner to do the dirty job.

Not knowing what else to do, Kathryn went to Sledge's dressing room and decided to wait for him there. So much was at stake.

Sledge didn't need her to fight his battles, she told herself, sinking down onto his sofa. He would simply refuse to change his name, throw a few choice words in Renfroe's face to put him in his place, and it would all be over. And no one would be hurt.

She settled back against the couch and realized that Sledge had been fighting Renfroe all the way by simply not heeding any of his advice. He was his own man. He had been since the day she'd met him. She wondered if that was what had made her love him.

Closing her eyes, she backed up in time and tried to remember the first moment her heart had been lost. Had it been the night of the party? No, she thought, it had happened before that. The morning she'd shaved off his mustache? No. She had lost the reins of her heart the moment their eyes had met in the bar.

A swirl of laughter pushed up through her chest as she remembered how adamantly she had planned to straighten him out. She had walked into this very room with him, declined his sarcastic offer to redecorate, got jealous over a picture of his sister...

Kathryn caught her breath as she saw an addition to the photos hanging on Sledge's wall. She got up and walked toward it. The new picture was the one of Sledge and Kathryn that had been in the newspaper. She smiled when she saw that Brad had been cut out of it. Sledge had once told her that he'd be a fool to hang a picture of one of his ladies on the wall. And now he had chosen Kathryn to be the one that he kept there.

Tears stung her eyes, and she wished she hadn't wasted so much time fighting him. She would make it up to him, she vowed silently. She would tell him—

The door burst open like an explosion, and Sledge stormed into the room. "What are you doing here?" he asked bitterly. "Gloating? Hanging around to see the results of your latest idea?"

Kathryn swung around and took in the chilling new emotion in his eyes. "Sledge, you don't understand. The name change wasn't—"

"There isn't going to be a name change." He jerked a box out of his closet and began dropping clothes into it. "For once you didn't get what you wanted. So you can go somewhere else and start over on your little creation."

The accusation stunned her, infuriated her. "You think *I* concocted that scheme? You think it was *my* idea?"

"I don't know why I didn't see it earlier," he said angrily, as he continued to shove things into his box. "You never wanted me. You never wanted any real man. You wanted someone you could mold and change. But you couldn't change me, so you changed my clothes and my hair and my face. And when that wasn't enough you decided to change my name!"

He stormed to the bathroom and opened the medicine cabinet to clear it out, too. "My ego, you said! You thought it was too inflated. Well, let me tell you something! You're the one with the ego problem. Anybody who thinks no one is good enough for her unless she's made him over needs serious help!"

"Sledge, stop it! You don't know what you're talking about!"

"Oh, don't I? You think I don't know that you've been playing some kind of Pygmalion game with me? But it's over, lady. Because I just quit this lousy job! I don't need this. I don't need Renfroe, and I don't need you!"

He began furiously grabbing photographs from the wall. When he came to the newest one, the one of the two of them, he held it to Kathryn's face to make certain she saw it. "And I don't need this anymore, either!" He sent the picture flying into an aluminum wastebasket. The glass shattered her heart with the impact.

Kathryn batted at the tears streaking her face and drew a deep, sobbing breath. "Sledge, you can't believe I had anything to do with—"

"Save it!" he shouted on his way out the door. "I was a fool to fall in love with you! And I'll pay for it. But I'm not going to be kicked around anymore."

Love? Had he said "love," as if it were the vilest of emotions? Kathryn buried her face in her hands, shaking her head violently. "You're wrong! You're—"

"Don't let it get you down," Sledge said. "Maybe you'll have better luck with your next victim!"

The door slammed behind him, quaking Kathryn's world, leaving her alone in the shambles. And she knew the pieces would never be put back together again.

CHAPTER ELEVEN

KATHRYN DIDN'T KNOW how much time had passed before her wailing thoughts ordered themselves. There was no point in being hurt over the cruel things Sledge had said to her. She had deserved them, she told herself. What else was he supposed to think? Knowing Renfroe, he'd likely made it sound as if the name change had been her brainstorm. All she had given Sledge the entire time they'd known each other was criticism. She'd used it to fight her renegade feelings, and now they were turning on her.

Wiping her face with hands trembling so hard that she was surprised they still functioned, she took a deep breath. First things first, she decided. She'd set things straight with Renfroe and try to get Sledge to take his job back. He belonged at the station, and as long as she had breath in her lungs, she would not let him walk away from it. Then she'd go after him to prove that she wasn't out to remake him. She'd go after him, praying that he would still have enough softness in his heart to believe her. And then she would find a way to convince him that she loved him and wasn't letting him go.

Before she had time to lose her nerve, she stepped out into the hall and marched to Renfroe's office doorway.

He was slumped over his desk, covering his face with his hands, shaking his head as though he couldn't believe what had happened. "Well, you took care of that, didn't you? And used me as your scapegoat when it blew up in your face."

Renfroe peered at her over his fingertips. "So sue me! I did what I thought would work. I thought if I told him it was your idea it would carry more weight."

"It carried weight, all right," Kathryn bit out. "Renfroe, you have some kind of nerve."

He clasped his hands behind his head and settled his elbows on his desk. "I'm in a bad mood, Kathryn. What do you want me to say? Uncle?"

Kathryn didn't know why his personality continually surprised her. "I want to try to get Sledge to come back here, because I think it's where he belongs. I want some guarantees to give him."

Renfroe looked doomed. "He won't come. He's fit to be tied, and I don't think we'll ever talk him into coming back. Which means we're done for. Without him *InSight* is sunk. And so am I."

"He'll come back on his terms," she said, hoping she was right. "But you'll have to let him follow his own instincts. No more changes. No more surprises."

Renfroe threw up his hands and bounced back on his swivel chair. "Fine! You've got me in a corner. My job is on the line here, you know! I just found out the big brass liked his tapes the way they were. And here I was just trying to improve on them. When they find out he's gone I'm finished."

Kathryn had no sympathy. "You'll have to let him wear whatever he sees fit. He has good taste. He knows what suits him."

"Who cares what he wears? He can wear a choir robe and go barefoot for all I care!"

"And let him wear his hair the way he likes it."

"Whatever," Renfroe said, nodding frantically.

"And the mustache is an absolute necessity."

Renfroe arched his brows and threw a glance heavenward, as if he realized he was being punished. "We'll give him everything else."

"He won't come back without that mustache." She crossed her arms and waited.

"No mustache!" Renfroe blurted, slapping the desk. "I have to draw the line somewhere."

"Fine," she said unyieldingly. "Draw your line. Draw it right through the time slot for *InSight*. Because there won't be a show if he doesn't get his mustache."

"All right!" the man bellowed. "Give him the godforsaken mustache. Let him grow a beard if he wants to. Just get him back here before the powers that be throw me out on the street!"

"I'll do what I can," Kathryn said. "And by the way, you and the powers that be will have a letter of resignation from me on your desks the first thing tomorrow."

"Oh, hell, Kathryn! Not you, too!"

"Me, too," she said. "I'm tired of changing people who shouldn't be changed, and I'm tired of following network orders I don't agree with and having my name used against me. That wasn't what I spent all my years of study for.''

''But think of all the money you'll be walking away from...''

''I'll manage on my own,'' she assured him. ''I've done it before.''

''But Kathryn—''

''I'll let you know as soon as I talk to Sledge,'' she said, and then she left the man moaning into his massive arms.

Kathryn made a point of getting Sledge's address from the receptionist before leaving the network building for the last time. As she drove numbly toward the photography studio to pick up the poster that seemed so insignificant now, she felt an empty sense of not belonging anywhere. What a mess everything was, she thought. One minute her career was skyrocketing, and the next, she didn't know how she'd pay her bills. One minute Sledge was calling her his lady, and the next, he was screaming accusations at her. One minute she was at the pinnacle of love, and the next she was crushed beneath a devastating avalanche. Where would it end?

When she reached the photographers', she went in and retrieved the poster. The cocky pose would have made her laugh if it hadn't reinforced the absurdity of her position. She was exactly where she'd said she wanted to be—out of Sledge's life. Only now she had two cardboard posters to remind her of the love that had almost been.

Not certain what to do with the poster now, she reclined the passenger seat of her car and put the poster there. Then she drove out of Manhattan and into the suburb where Sledge lived. It took her a while to find the street she had written down, and when she did, she was certain she'd made the journey in vain. Impossible, she thought. This couldn't be the home of the Darryl Sledge she knew.

Kathryn pulled into the circular driveway and got out of her car, staring, flabbergasted, at the house nestled in the modest residential area. She tried to pinpoint what she had expected. A chrome-and-glass bachelor pad? A hot tub on the front lawn? An imported sports car in the driveway? Instead she saw a quaint house set smack in the middle of a neighborhood sprinkled with children, with azaleas blooming in the garden.

Two little boys played in the backyard, running in and out of a well-constructed fort on which was nailed a sign that read Private—Keep Out. One of them bolted forward at the sight of her.

"Swedge isn't home," he informed her.

She smiled at the mispronunciation of Sledge's name and breathed a sigh of relief that she had, at least, come to the right house. "And who are you?"

"Wusty," the little boy said. "I wiv next door. Swedge built us that fort and said we could pway there even when he's gone."

She stood up and looked at the fort, which had been constructed with quite a bit of care. "He built that for you?"

"For me and some other guys. We have a cwub, you know."

Kathryn smiled. "Rusty, have you seen Swedge—I mean, Sledge—today?"

The little boy shrugged and shook his head.

Then he hadn't come straight home, Kathryn realized, and again she was left with no idea of where to look for him. If she had to go home and wait for him, she could at least leave him a note.

A note—and her poster! She smiled a half smile and looked down at the little boy. "If you see Sledge, tell him Kathy came by. I'm going to leave him something in his garage. Make sure he sees it, all right?"

"Okay." The little boy waved goodbye and dashed back to the fort.

Quickly Kathryn pulled out the poster and stood it up in the garage, just inside the door. Then she searched her car and purse for paper, but found none. Giving up, she decided to write what had to be said on the T-shirt portion of the poster. Writing as fast as she could move her pen, she explained that she'd had nothing to do with the name change, that the network had offered him everything he wanted to make him come back and that she, too, was unemployed. And then she wrote that she loved him, and signed it: "One heart for another, Kathy."

She hurried home and waited—hours, it seemed—but Sledge never called. Feeling nauseous and wilted, she took a shower, forced herself to eat and went to sit beside the mute phone again.

When darkness filled the room, she went to bed and lay staring at the ceiling, wondering where he could be. Had he left town? Gone back to Texas? Had he gone for good?

She tried Dallas information, found no listing for Sledge. Then, grasping for straws, she called the television station he'd worked for previously. They had not heard from him.

Uncertainty ate at her into the night, stealing hope and feeding that unfathomable void that had been yawning within her since she'd met Sledge. And when she started to cry, she was certain that as long as she lived the tears would never stop.

What if he had come back and hadn't bothered getting in touch with her after reading her note? What if he'd decided her stubbornness was too big an obstacle between them? She felt so helpless. . . .

Darkness encompassed her like a cold black hole, a pit from which there was no escape, and for the first time in her life she was afraid to sleep without the light.

But even with the lamp on, sleep would not come. She got out of bed, crossed the room in her long pink nightgown and went to the sliding glass doors of the balcony. Opening them, she stepped outside, and felt the rush of midsummer wind warm her.

The moon was full in an onyx sky, mocking the state of anyone foolish enough to be alone tonight. Kathryn sat on the concrete patio and leaned her head against the wrought-iron railing, praying that she had not lost Sledge forever.

Like a never-ending film in a plaguing nightmare, moments with Sledge played in her mind. The vulnerable look in his eyes when she'd shaved off his mustache, the glint of mischief in them when he'd made her buy the leopard-skin briefs, the pain in them when he'd declared his love as he walked out on her.

Another tear rolled slowly down her face, and a soul-deep sigh tore out of her.

She heard a light rap at the door, and caught her breath, pushing a sudden surge of hope to the back of her mind. It wasn't Sledge. It was Amanda, she told herself, eager to hear what Sledge's reaction had been to the poster.

Kathryn wiped away the evidence of her tears and closed the sliding doors behind her, then padded slowly across the floor. The knock came again.

She twisted the bolt and opened the door.

The sight she saw across the threshold made her collapse against the wall in relief, and she clamped her hands over her mouth as fresh tears rushed to her eyes. The original Darryl Sledge had indeed returned to haunt her.

Sledge was leaning against the doorjamb, wearing nothing but a relieved grin and a pair of antique jeans, his legs crossed at the ankles in cowboy boots, and that black Stetson hanging from his fingers. The day's stubble shaded the space above lips that were curved in a soft, seductive smile. "Don't look so scared," he whispered with a tremor in his voice. "It's just me." He swallowed and took a deep breath. "I have a little problem with my image," he rumbled in a drawl that was the most beautiful sound she'd ever heard. "Heard you worked miracles."

She swallowed and wiped her blurry eyes. "You can't fix something that isn't broken," she whispered.

His eyes misted over, and he tapped his chest. "How about broken hearts? Can you fix those?"

She breathed a soft laugh that came out as a sob. "You bet I can."

His arms came around her, and his kiss was instant—hungry, soft, demanding, gentle, ravishing, sweet—all at once. His arms enfolded her in a crushing embrace, and she felt her feet leaving the floor. For all she cared, she could have been hurling through space, never to touch earth again as long as she had Darryl Sledge to hold on to.

She basked in the warmth in his eyes when he broke the kiss. "I love you," she whispered.

"Say it again," he entreated, loosening his hold and letting her slide down his body until her feet touched the floor. "Say it over and over and over. . . ."

"I love you—I love you—I love you," she breathed against his neck as her tears ran down his bare chest and flirted with the dark, curling hair there. "Where have you been?"

He laced his fingers through her hair. "Sitting in the airport for half the day, trying to decide whether to go back to Texas. Then sitting on the bank of the Hudson, feeling sorry for myself because I couldn't seem to get on that plane." His lips crushed hers again, his intoxicating kiss testing for affirmation that she had really surrendered. "And when I came back and saw that wonderful poster and your note—God, I must have broken the sound barrier getting over here."

Kathryn ran her fingers over his unshaved face, memorizing the rugged lines and rough texture. "Renfroe wants you back at any cost."

Sledge smirked and looked skeptical. "So you said in the note. Does that include keeping my name?"

"He said at any cost."

"Sure," he said dubiously.

"Even the mustache," she said. "I told him it was an absolute necessity."

A slow grin skittered across his face, and he set his cowboy hat on her head. "My mustache, huh? Well, I'll think about it. What about you? Will you go back?"

"No," she said. "From now on I'm going to help people who need help. I'll choose my clients, and I'll do what I set out to do at the beginning of my career. No more Renfroes to take orders from."

"And no more bullheaded Sledges to resist."

"I could never resist you," she told him.

"I resisted you, though. At least professionally. I made your life pretty hard there for a while."

"You fought for yourself, and I'm thankful you did. If you hadn't, I might have turned you into a Brad Miller and lost something vitally important to me. I fell in love with the original Sledge."

"And I would have lost you when you left after your work on me was over. I knew what I was doing."

He sat down on the couch and pulled her onto his lap. His azure eyes grew serious, eloquent, and she saw his throat convulse with emotion.

"How would you feel..."

She buried her fingers in his hair and pressed a soft kiss on his lips.

"About spending the rest of your life..."

She kissed his eyelids, one at a time.

"With a guy who has absolutely nothing going for him..."

She ran her tongue over his upper lip, feeling the velvety brush of a mustache in the making.

"Except that he's sexy..."

She smiled and nuzzled his neck.

"Good-looking..."

She shivered at the feel of his breath against her neck and nibbled her way to his ear.

"Intelligent..."

She ran her hand down his bare chest, savoring the feel of his heart beating out his love.

"And has a smile that invokes palpitations and invites astrological talk and name calling from ladies young and old?"

A ribbon of laughter curled out from the depths of Kathryn's throat.

He issued a heavy sigh. "Somehow I don't think you're taking me too seriously."

She traced a circle around his granuled nipple. "I seriously think I could manage to love a guy with so little going for him," she whispered breathlessly, pulling him down with her as she lay back on the couch.

"You do know we're talking marriage," he said, falling down with her.

"Of course," she said happily as he began to open her nightgown. "Our posters can stand up for us at the wedding."

He chuckled against her ear and started working the gown over one shoulder, his lips blazing a trail to her swelling breasts. "No, you aren't taking this seriously at all."

"I am," she whispered. "It's just that I was wondering if I'd be marrying a Sledge or a Saxon."

"Does it matter?" he teased. "As long as you know that I'm Darryl...."

"Hi, Darryl," she said saucily, and then her lips brushed his, soft and wet, in a kiss that revealed her growing desire. With a playful circle of her tongue, she pulled back, brushing her lips over his again. "How am I doing?" she whispered.

"Good," he said with a grin. "But I was trying to tell you, I'm Darryl Sledge—"

"Hi, Darryl Sledge," she said. Her lips crushed his, and a wondrous sigh escaped his lungs as he held her tightly against him.

"You want to go for the middle name?" she asked, breaking the kiss.

He touched his lips to her forehead. "Don't think I don't know what you're up to," he teased.

Her eyes sparkled mischievously as she continued the game they had started in the bar the first night, the night that had changed their lives. "Ah, but awareness is no defense against my techniques," she whispered. "And there's so much to do. Problem is, knowing where to begin. But don't worry. I love challenges."

He laughed aloud and settled over her, anchoring her with his weight. "Then you'll enjoy the hell out of me," he drawled.

"My unpolished Texas man," she whispered in misty awe of the love flowing between them. "Do I really have an exclusive?"

He reached out to take the Stetson off of her head and set it on his own at a rakish angle. "To do with as you wish, ma'am."

The phone rang just as he was about to rid her completely of the garment in his way. She caught his hand as he reached over to answer it.

"Don't," she said.

Sledge withdrew his hand and framed her face lovingly. He kissed her, sparking her into flaming life as the answering machine clicked on and her sister's excited voice filled the room.

"Kat," Amanda cried. "Is it okay to wear red satin to your own wedding? Okay, so it's decadent, but white makes me look so pale. Oh, and what do you think of rhinestone fingernails? The kind you stick on. By the way, I'm going to be Mrs. Brad Miller. Did I tell you that?"

Sledge and Kathryn broke into spontaneous laughter as the machine clicked off. "What are we going to do with her?" Kathryn asked.

"Question is," he answered, his eyes growing intent, making her senses scream in anticipation, "what am I going to do with you?"

A daring sparkle shone in her eyes as she raised her arms invitingly. "I'm putty," she said. "Mold away."

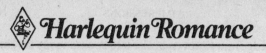

Harlequin Romance

Coming Next Month

2797 BOSS OF YARRAKINA Valerie Parv
A sham engagement for the sake of her aunt's health is one thing; marriage, quite another. And Joselin goes out of her way to avoid tying the knot with the boss of Yarrakina—only to discover he truly is the man for her.

2798 THE LAST BARRIER Edwina Shore
In Scotland, a young woman who's still overwhelmed by the accident that killed her fiancé, resists when her heart goes out to a young orphan and to the boy's disturbing uncle.

2799 ONE LIFE AT A TIME Natalie Spark
The search is over, but her problems are just beginning. She's found the man she fell in love with three years ago—the man who'd lost his memory. Only he seems to have forgotten her.

2800 SO NEAR, SO FAR Jessica Steele
A secretary's new boss lectures her about her reputation with men and insists he won't be taken in by her wiles. Now how can she make him like her without confirming his worst suspicions?

2801 AUTUMN IN APRIL Essie Summers
The nerve of the man! She and his grandfather had discussed love. Not money. The undying love the older man had felt for her grandmother—the kind of love Matthieu obviously didn't understand.

2802 BREAKING FREE Marcella Thompson
Admittedly, this city slicker knows nothing about farming. But she intends to fulfill her poultry contract with Clear Creeks Farm in Arkansas—if only to show the arrogant owner what she's made of.

Available in November wherever paperback books are sold, or through Harlequin Reader Service.

In the U.S.
P.O. Box 1397
Buffalo, N.Y.
14240-1397

In Canada
P.O. Box 2800, Postal Station A
5170 Yonge Street
Willowdale, Ontario M2N 6J3

Take 4 novels and a surprise gift FREE

Where passion and destiny meet . . . there is love

Jesse's Lady
Veronica Sattler

Brianna Deveraux had a feisty spirit matched by that of only one man, Jesse Randall. In North Carolina, 1792, they dared to forge a love as vibrant and alive as life in their bold new land.

Available at your favorite bookstore in SEPTEMBER, or reserve your copy for August shipping. Send your name, address, zip or postal code with a check or money order for $5.25 (includes 75¢ for postage and handling) payable to Worldwide Library Reader Service to:

In the U.S.	In Canada
Worldwide Library	Worldwide Library
901 Fuhrmann Blvd.	P.O. Box 2800, 5170 Yonge St.
Box 1325	Postal Station A
Buffalo, New York	Willowdale, Ontario
14269-1325	M2N 6J3

PLEASE SPECIFY BOOK TITLE WITH YOUR ORDER.

JES-H-1